69 AND STILL ALIVE

BURL SORENSON

ISBN 978-1-63784-330-7 (paperback)
ISBN 978-1-63784-331-4 (digital)

Hawes & Jenkins Publishing
16427 N Scottsdale Road Suite 410
Scottsdale, AZ 85254
www.hawesjenkins.com

Printed in the United States of America

CHAPTER 1

There were two hip dudes named Burl Johnson and Duke. Duke was sixty-nine years old while Burl was sixty-four years old but was looking forward to turning sixty-nine, the love number. They were both chefs, and they cooked up some really mean shit. Duke's specialty was brick oven pizza. Burl's specialty was Italian because he had been to Sorrento, Italy, with his gorgeous wife, Audrey. Burl was heavyset, about six feet three inches, 225 pounds, bulky, blond hair, and emerald-green eyes. Duke, on the other hand, was stocky about five feet eleven inches, 185 pounds, black hair, and ice-blue eyes. Both were well-tanned.

Duke and Burl thought they were bad as shit. They would later air on *Bon Appetite*, an awesome cooking show.

Duke, at one point, went noodling in Oklahoma. He would shove his hand into some subaquatic underbrush and pull out a huge catfish, probably a two-pounder. Then he tried his luck with his foot and pulled out a five-pounder. Duke was proud of his accomplishment.

Having had enough of noodling, the two then headed down to Louisiana to nail some alligators. They cruised out to the Bayou with a cat named Earl on his Mercury twin-engine one-hundred-horse-power Bayliner, center console. Luck was tilting their way that day.

On his first try, Earl landed an estimated nine-pounder. Then Earl pulled out his net and cast it into the water and pulled in what was probably a thirty-pounder.

Duke then bellowed out, "Hey, Earl, let me have at it." A huge gator jumped about ten feet out of the water.

"Burl, look at that motherfucker. I'm gonna nail it with the net," Burl yelled out.

Duke cast the net into the water, and moments later, he landed the gator. "About a three hundred pounder."

"Fuck, look at those boys. Biggest one that we've caught thus far."

"Let me at it, Duke. I'm gonna catch one bigger than that," said Burl.

Burl then cast the net out, and sure enough, he landed into a big one; and Duke and Earl pulled it with all their might into the boat.

"Look at that this boy. This is the biggest motherfucker we've caught thus far. Must weigh about four hundred pounds," said Earl.

The three of them went back to Earl's crib on Bourbon Street in New Orleans.

Earl skinned the gators in a flash. Paul Prudhomme, a renowned New Orleans chef, would have been so proud of the boys.

Earl sliced the gator meat into one-pound fillets. Then took their catch down to the Garden District to Jacques's fine eatery, a restaurant known to serve the finest gator in town. Jacque, the proprietor, was so amazed and gave Earl one thousand bucks (since he was the boat's captain) and Duke and Burl five hundred bucks each.

So elated were Duke and Burl that they then went down to Bourbon Street to pick up a couple of hookers. But first, they decided that they wanted to listen to some good music.

They first went into a joint called Blues Alley where B. B. King was jamming. Burl was an awesome guitarist; he'd played with the likes of Muddy Waters and John Lee Hooker.

B. B. invited Burl up on stage to jam with him. They then belted out a rendition of "The Thrill Is Gone," one that B. B. wrote, as well as "The Statesboro Blues," a tune written by the Allman Brothers Band, and "In Memory of Elizabeth Reed," also written by the Allman Brothers.

They then did a rendition of "Hey Joe," written by Jimmy Hendrix and Roy Buchanan. Burl picked and strummed the cords like a well-seasoned musician.

By then, Duke and Burl were hungry as shit; so they cruised down to the Reverend's restaurant on Layfette Street to chow down on some crawfish, frog legs, and oysters on the half shell—cuisine the Reverend's was renowned for. The money and booze flowed freely that night.

The two of them then headed down to chow down on some good Italian food.

They entered the restaurant located on Sixty-Ninth and Canal Street, a rather posh joint.

A hostess approached them. "Good evening, gentlemen. My name's Sophia. How may I help you?"

"Hi, Sophia. We need a table for two, preferably in a booth by the window," said Burl.

Sophia then led them to their booth.

"Here you go, gentlemen, a table for two. Your waiter, his name's Guido, will be serving you this evening."

The two sat pensively for a few minutes, at which point Guido approached the table with the bottle of wine and two wine glasses.

"Here you go, gentlemen. Which of you two would like to sample it?"

Duke responded, "You go ahead, bro. I have no experience with this."

"Guess that I'll do the honors, Guido," said Burl.

Guido popped the cork and handed it to Burl.

The cork was wet, not dry, just as it should be.

"Cork's fine, Guido. Hit me with a shot of it."

"Certainly, sir," he responded. At that, he poured a small amount into Burl's wine glass. He swirled it around for several seconds allowing it to breathe a little and then took a sip.

"Excellent, Guido!"

"I thought that you'd like it, sir. I'll have your food out shortly."

"Now, what would you two like to order?"

"What's your suggestion, Guido?"

"Well, the lobster ravioli is very good, usually served al dente drizzled with a splash of rosé wine. I'd suggest the 1869 vintage from Sicily."

"I'll go with that," replied Burl.

"And you, sir, what would you like to eat?"

"I was thinking of the spaghetti and meatballs with sweet Italian sausage."

"Aah, an excellent choice. How would you like your pasta cooked?"

"I'd like it al dente as well."

"Would you like any wine with your dinner?"

"Yes, I was thinking about a merlot. What would you suggest?"

"The 1969 vintage from Milan is an excellent choice."

"Thank you, Guido, I'll go with that," replied Duke.

"Oh, one more thing, Guido. Could you please serve us some garlic bread along with the meal and some tomato compress?" asked Burl.

"By all means." At that, Guido was off to the kitchen.

"My girl, Audrey, she really knows her shit about wine and fine cuisine for that matter."

"Bro, this is the best fucking wine I've ever tasted. How'd you know it was so good? By the way, how's your girl doing? I've never met her."

"Dude, she's the best woman in the world. You just gotta meet her."

"When will that be, bro?"

"Probably not for a bit. She's in school right now."

"Oh yeah, what school is she in?"

"Mount St. Mary's University in Emmitsburg, MD."

"What's she majoring in?"

"Business and finance. The girl's smart as shit."

"Think you'll marry her?"

"Probably so once I finish school."

"What school you at, bro?"

"You should know dude, St. Mary's College in St. Mary's City, MD."

"Whaddya majoring in?"

"Genetics and molecular biology."

"Are you liking it?" asked Duke.

"Bro, I love the shit out of it."

"Oh yeah, how so?"

"Man, you learn everything about your inheritance and ancestry. I'm learning all this cool shit. I'm learning about Gregor Mendel and his experiments with peas and fruit flies and dominant and recessive traits. In molecular biology, I'm learning about DNA synthesis, RNA synthesis, transcription, translation, and protein synthesis. In fact, I can't wait to get back at it."

"Man, that's all above my head," said Duke.

"How about you, Duke? Any plans on attending college?"

"Yeah, in fact, I have. I'm thinking that I'd like to major in pharmacology. I could learn how to synthesize cocaine, uppers, and downers, all that shit. You know of any schools that offer that curriculum?"

"Yeah, the University of Maryland at Baltimore [UMAB]."

"Dude, my sister, Ange, is studying nursing there."

"Really, bro?"

"Yeah man, just think, you'd have somebody to hang out with."

"I've never met Ange. Is she cool?"

"Yeah, man, she's the best. In high school, we used to smoke weed together, do uppers, downers, and all that shit."

"Really, when can I meet her?"

"Pretty soon, bro. Just let me get through visiting with the fam. And I'll have you over for dinner, lunch, or some such shit."

"Cool, cool, cool." At that moment, the food arrived.

"Here you go, gentlemen. Spaghetti for you my friend and ravioli for you, sir, and here's your garlic bread. Anything else?"

"Yes, sir, can you please serve us the tomato compress?"

"Great. I'll get right on it enjoy!" And that they did.

Several minutes later, Guido returned with the tomato compress.

"Here you go, gentlemen. Can I get you anything else?"

"No thanks," said Burl. "I think we're all set."

"Great. If you do need anything else, just flag down the busboy."

"Will do, Guido," Duke replied.

The two ate voraciously.

"Dude, this is the best ravioli I've ever tasted," said Duke.

"I told you so, bro. You can't go wrong with Sabatini's."

The meal took about forty-five minutes for them to complete, at which point Guido approached their table again.

"How was the meal, gentlemen?" he asked.

"Excellent," the two responded.

"May I get you anything else?"

"Do you have tiramisu?" Burl asked.

"So long as the pope is Catholic, we sure do."

"Great. We'll take two if you don't mind."

"You got it." At that, Guido was off to the kitchen.

"Bro, how'd you learn so much about fine dining?" Duke asked.

"From my girl, Audrey. Her mother was Italian."

"Man, you gotta stick by Audrey. She sounds like a really cool chick."

"You got that right, bro. There's no fucking way I'm giving her up, not in a million years."

"When can I meet her dude?"

"How about next week?" If you come out to the restaurant, you can meet her then."

"What restaurant you are working at?"

"The Family Fish House, you know, it's located on East Jefferson Street in Rockville."

"Yeah, bro, I know exactly where that is."

"You know that it's an all-you-can-eat joint. I'll feed you to the gills with seafood."

"What kinda food?"

"Dude, they got everything. Fried clams, fried flounder, Alaskan crab legs, frog legs, and steamed shrimp. Also, serve hush puppies."

"You gotta date, bro."

"Is Audrey a waitress?"

"Naw, man, she's a hostess. A hostess with the mostess, I might add."

"Cool, bro, I'll make a date of it. What day works best for you?"

"Probably Friday or Saturday night."

"Can I bring anyone else along?"

"Sure."

"Cool. Think I'll invite Tommy, Rich, and Russell."

"That's cool. Why don't you come in around 7:00 p.m."

"You gotta deal."

At that, they both chowed down to their hearts' delight. After dinner, they headed back to Burl's crib in Fells Point. They woke up the next morning around nine.

"How'd you sleep, bro?" Burl asked Duke.

"Like a fucking champ, man. That food at Sabatini's put me right to sleep."

"Whaddya want to do today?" Duke asked.

"The Orioles are playing the Red Sox tonight. Wanna go to the game?"

"Fuck yeah, man! Especially since the O's have a shot at the pennant."

"What time's the game?"

"At 7:05 p.m."

"Wanna catch a bite before the game?" Duke asked.

"Definitely, bro."

"Where you thinking?"

"You like mussels?"

"Do I like mussels? Fuck yeah, dude."

"Great, then we'll go to Bertha's Mussels." At that, the two crashed out for the night.

Tired, they slept for a full twelve hours and woke up at 1:00 p.m.

"What do you want to do for lunch?" Burl asked Duke. "The game's not on until 7:05 p.m."

"Jack's Deli. It's on Sixty-Ninth and Eastern Avenue."

"You like corned beef?"

"Fucking 'A.'"

"Great, then we'll go down to Jack's Deli. They serve the best Reubens in town."

They both got dressed and headed down to Jack's at about two thirty.

Burl had been to the restaurant numerous times and knew the staff well. Jack, the proprietor was working behind the counter.

"Hey, Jack, how goes it?" Burl asked.

"Fine, Burl. How about you?"

"Doing great Jack, thanks for asking. Anything on special for today?"

"Got pretty much the usual, Burl. I do know you like the Reubens, but I am trying out corned beef on sourdough bread. Not sure how well it'll take off. Who's your friend?"

"Oh, this is Duke. Duke Stevens."

"Pleased to meet you, Duke."

"Me as well."

"Please have a seat, gentleman. Your waitress will be right with you."

"Thanks, Jack," Burl said.

The place was furnished with typical Americana: red checkered tablecloths, pine chairs, and flowers on each table.

Their waitress approached them.

"Hi, fellas. What can I get you? By the way, my name's Jill. I'll be waiting on you today."

"Great, Jill. I'll have a National Bohemian."

"I'll have the same," Duke replied.

"Now, what can I get you to eat?"

"I'll take the Reuben," Burl replied.

"I'll try out the corned beef on sourdough bread."

"Cool. Jack will be interested if you like it or not."

"You got it." At that, Jill left the table.

"Bro, check out Jill's ass."

"Dude, you gotta get your mind out of the gutter. Jack's a good friend of mine, and I don't want us to get kicked out of the restaurant."

"Sorry, man, I'll chill out."

"Order up," Jack belted out.

A few moments later, Jill approached their table.

"Here you go, fellas. Anything else?"

"Nope," Burl responded. "I think we're okay for now."

"Enjoy."

"Bro, I'm really glad that we're back in Baltimore, New Orleans, was enough for a few days."

CHAPTER 2

The two finished their meal around 4:00 p.m. and then headed back to Burl's crib on 69 Broadwood Street in Fells Point; they arrived at around 4:30 p.m.

They entered Burl's crib, and Burl exclaimed. "Hey, Duke, wanna smoke some weed? We've got that Colombian red that Smoking Joe sold us.

"Bro, let's fire up a bowl," he replied.

At that, Burl headed into his bedroom to retrieve the chamber pipe that Joe had sold them and then returned to the living room.

"Fire up that bitch!" Duke belted out.

"Here, dude, you do the honors."

"Sure thing, buddy," he replied.

Duke pulled out his Zippo lighter and fired up the bowl. He took a huge pull on the pipe and held the smoke in for several seconds and then exhaled.

"Bro, this shit's the fucking bomb."

"No shit," Burl replied. "Let me hit it."

"Sure thing, brother."

Burl also took a huge pull on the pipe, held it in for several seconds, and then exhaled the smoke.

"Man, you weren't kidding. This is some really good shit."

"Dude, I know. Joe really did us justice!"

"Bro, I got the munchies!" Burl exclaimed. "Let's head out to Bertha's."

"Dude, I'm on it. Let's head out."

It was about 5:00 p.m. when the two arrived at Bertha's. Upon entering, they were approached by a hostess.

"Good evening, gentlemen. How may I help you?"

"We'd like a table for two if you don't mind."

"Don't mind at all, please follow me."

The hostess seated them at a two-top located in the corner.

"Is this okay, gentleman?"

"This will do just fine," Duke replied.

"Great. Your waitress will be right with you."

They perused the menu.

"What're you thinking of ordering, Burl?" Duke asked.

"Mussels, what'd you think."

"I know, bro, but which kind?"

"I'm thinking the Mexican ones. They're made with cumin and Mexican chili powder and finished off with a shot of Jose Cuervo tequila.

"Sounds good, bro, Any suggestions for me?"

"Dude, I tell you, the Italian ones are awesome. I had them the last time I was here."

"Oh yeah, how do they fix them?"

"Don't quite remember, but all their mussels are excellent. You can't go wrong with any of them."

"Cool, then that's what I'll get."

Moments later, a waitress approached their table.

"Good evening, gentlemen, my name's Melissa. I'll be your server for the evening. May I start you off with something to drink?"

"Sure thing," replied Burl. "Do you by chance have Stein 69 malt liquor?"

"Sure do, would you like that in a bottle or a glass?"

"I'll take a pint of that if you have it."

"Sure do. How about you, sir?" she asked Duke.

"I'll have the same," he replied.

"Are you ready to order the main course?"

"Sure are," replied Burl.

"So what'll it be?"

"I'd like the Mexican mussels," replied Burl.

"I'll take the Italian ones," replied Duke.

"Thanks, Melissa, I think that'll do it," replied Duke.

"Great. Your order should be ready in about twenty minutes." At that, Melissa took off to the kitchen to fill their order.

"Bro, look at that cute little ass swaying from side to side, and her tits must be a 36D cup."

"Dude, is that all you can think of these days?"

"Man, I haven't been laid since our visit to New Orleans, and the bitch I banged was skanky as shit," replied Duke.

"Sorry, bro, I feel for you."

"Ready for the O's game tonight?"

"Am I ever. Hope that they beat the shit out of the Red Sox."

"Well, they're up three games to zero in the playoffs if they win this one it's off to the World Series."

"You know who's in the lineup for tonight?"

"Yeah, I think Palmer's pitching, Brooks Robinson at third, Frank Robinson in left field, and Boog Powell at first base."

"Know who's catching?"

"Probably Paul Casanova."

"Cool. Given that lineup, they should have no problem winning the game."

"Sure hope so," Burl replied.

A few minutes later, Melissa arrived with their beer.

"Here you go, gentlemen, two Stein 69s. Your food should be ready shortly."

"Thank you," Duke replied.

"Yeah, thanks Melissa," Burl said.

Duke raised his glass.

"To the good life good buddy." He spoke.

"Cheers to that," Burl replied.

Frosty pints in hand, they both took a gulp of their beer.

"Man, this is some good shit," replied Duke.

"Got that right buddy," said Burl.

Several minutes later, they both had finished their beer and were ready for seconds.

Burl flagged down the busboy.

"Hello, my friend, could you please ask Melissa over to our table?"

"Sure thing. I'll get her right away."

Several minutes later, Melissa approached their table. "Another round, boys?" she asked.

"Sure thing," replied Duke.

"Gotcha covered," she replied, and off she was to the bar.

"So when you gonna see Audrey?"

"Tomorrow, bro. I'm heading back to Rockville and am gonna hang out at my folks for a few days."

"Wanna go to the restaurant tomorrow night?"

"Sure. What time you thinking?" asked burl.

"How about 7:00 p.m.?"

"Sounds good to me. I'll call Tommy, Rich, and Russell and let them know."

"Cool."

Several minutes later, Melissa appeared with their order. "Mexican mussels for you and Italian mussels for you, my friend."

"Thanks, Melissa," they both replied.

"No problem, gentlemen. Enjoy."

At that, the two proceeded to chow down.

"Man, these fucking mussels are the best," said Duke.

"I know, bro. I told you so."

They finished eating around 6:00 p.m.

"Dude, we gotta get legs. The game starts in about an hour.

"Alright, alright, I'm finishing up now," Duke said.

"Cool," said Burl.

"Should we walk to the game?" Duke asked.

"Naw, bro, it's too far. We'll have to catch a cab."

The two then step outside the restaurant and hailed a cab. It was a Cruise Along cab, number 69.

They both step into the cab. The driver was an East Indian named Mukesh as listed on the headrest in front of Burl and one of those funky seat covers made out of wooden balls or some such shit.

"Where to, gentlemen?" he asked.

"Camden Yards. We're checking out tonight's game."

"Very, very good. I'll get you there right away."

It was a short drive to the stadium.

"Here you go, gentlemen. Enjoy the game. That'll be $30."

"Whoa, $30? You gotta be kidding," said Duke. "You only drove us three fucking blocks."

"I'm so very sorry, but I don't make the rules."

"You got thirty bucks, Burl?"

"Yeah, but all I have is a Ben Franklin."

"Here you go, Mukesh, here's a hundred," said Burl.

"But, sir, I don't have change for that."

"Then tough shit, that's all I've got. Take it or leave it."

"Then I'll have to call the police on you."

"Fuck off, you dot head," said Duke.

"I don't appreciate being called a dot head," said Mukesh.

"So sorry, you motherfucker," said Burl. At that, the two climbed out of the cab without paying. They then approached the gate on Eutaw Street. The crowd was amassing outside the gate.

"Bro, take a look at the crowd. Never seen it this crowded," said Duke.

"Dude, I know. I guess it can be expected given the O's have a chance at the pennant."

Street vendors were outside the gate selling hats, T-shirts, and all sorts of memorabilia.

"I'm gonna grab me a T-shirt," said Burl. "You want one, bro? It's on me."

"Sure, man, thanks."

Burl headed up to the vendor. "I'll take two T-shirts," said Burl.

"What size you want?"

"Two XLs.

"You got it. That'll be fifty bucks."

"All I've got is a $100 bill. You got change for that?"

"Sure do, buddy." The vendor made change and handed the T-shirts to Burl. "Here you go, my friend."

"Thanks, man, appreciate it."

"No problem."

"Here you go, Duke."

"Thanks, bro. I'll cover you for the refreshments."

"Cool."

The two of them then headed inside the stadium.

"Where're seats, bro?"

"Section 69, upper deck."

"Cool. Let's head up there."

"Who's coaching the O's this year?" Duke asked.

"Earl Weaver," Burl replied.

"Man, I thought he was over the hill and retired a long time ago."

"No, bro, he's still kicking."

"Whaddya want to eat?" asked Duke.

"Think I'll get a bratwurst. What do you want?"

"Think I'll get a Boog's BBQ sandwich."

The two grabbed their food and headed out to their seats which were behind home plate.

"Bro, these are the best seats in the house. How much did you pay for them?"

"They weren't cheap, I paid $269 for the pair."

"Damn, I'll pay you for them."

"That's okay dude considers it an early birthday present."

"You sure, bro?"

"Yeah man, I'm sure."

"Cool, cool, cool."

"What year were you born, Duke?

"The year 1969."

"No kidding. I was born September 19, but it was 1959."

"Wish the game would start. What time is it?"

"Six fifty-nine. Should be starting in just a few minutes."

"Cool," said Duke.

As if on cue, the two teams took to the field.

"Palmer's getting old as shit. How many more years you think he's got left in him?"

"Don't know, bro, but if he keeps pitching the way he has lately, I'd say he still has a few more years left in him. You know he won the Cy Young award in '69. In his last game with the Yankees, he pitched a no-hitter."

"No fucking way."

"Yup, believe it or not, he did."

"Damn nation," Duke replied.

"How much longer you think Brooks and Frank Robinson will be around?"

"Now, that's a different story. I think they're both retiring this year."

"Really? That'll be the downfall of the O's."

"I disagree with you, bro. Look who they have coming up from the Rochester AAA farm league."

"Oh yeah, who they got?"

"Cal Ripken Jr., Eddie Murry, Billy Ripken, Tippy Martinez, and Rick Dempsey."

"Bro you're right, they're gonna be tough to beat."

"Dude, I told you so."

"No more talking. Here comes the first pitch."

Palmer threw a fastball at ninety-five miles per hour.

"Bro, did you see that? Ninety-five miles per hour. Palmer still has it."

"Yeah, man, he still has his shit together."

The game lasted for three hours. The O's won it, 6–0. They then headed back to Burl's crib.

"What time are you heading out in the morning?" Duke asked Burl.

"Pretty early. I'm thinking around 7:00 a.m."

"Too early for me, bro," Duke replied.

"When you gonna head out to Rockville?" Burl asked.

"Not until the afternoon."

"Cool, then I'll see you at the restaurant around 7:00 p.m."

CHAPTER 3

Burl went back to his crib and packed up enough clothes for a couple of days' stay at his folk's home.

About twenty minutes later, he headed out the door—destination, Rockville. An hour later he was at the doorsteps to his parent's home.

"Mom, Dad, I'm home.

"Oh, hello, Burl. Didn't think you were coming home today," Charlotte said.

"Yeah, Mom, I gotta work at the Fish House tonight."

"No worries, Burl. Don't get me wrong, it's so good to see you again."

"Where's Pops?"

"Downstairs in his woodshop."

"Great. I'm gonna say hi to him."

"Go right ahead, Burl." At that, he headed downstairs to the woodshop. "Morning, Pops. How's it going?

"Good, Burl. How're doing? Didn't think that you'd be home today."

"Mom just said the same thing, but I gotta work tonight."

"Where you are you working tonight, the Fish House or the country club?"

"Fish House."

"Great, then you'll have a chance to see Audrey."

"Yeah, Pops, I really can't wait to see Audrey. I miss her so very much."

"Audrey's a good woman, Burl. Make sure that you hang onto her."

"Believe me, Pops, I'm never gonna give her up."

"Glad to hear that, son. By the way, what's Mom cooking for dinner?"

"Not sure, Pops. Let me go ask her." Burl headed back upstairs. "Hey, Mom, Pops wants to know what we're having for dinner."

"Spinach and bacon quiche."

"Awesome, I absolutely love your quiche. Anything to go along with it?"

"Yes, we're having creamed corn, fresh from your father's garden."

"Great. I'll go tell Pops that." At that point, Burl headed back down to the woodshop."

"So, Burl, what're we having for dinner?"

"Spinach and bacon quiche along with creamed corn."

"Great. Your mom makes the best quiche."

"Don't I know it. By the way, Pops, how's the garden doing?"

"It's just about finished for the year."

"How'd it go this year?"

"Great. I harvested strawberries, tomatoes, cucumbers, green beans, peas, carrots, spinach, lettuce, yellow squash, zucchini, and corn."

"Wow! Sounds like a huge success."

"Best year that I've had in a long time. Please call me when dinner's ready, son."

"Sure will, Pops."

"By the way, you mind taking Sheba for a walk? She hasn't been walked in a while."

"Sure thing, Pops." Burl then headed back upstairs to the kitchen. "Mom, I'm gonna take Sheba for a walk."

"Go right ahead, Burl. Breakfast will be ready in about a half hour."

Burl headed out to the doghouse where Sheba slept. "Come on, girl, wanna go for a walk?"

Excitedly, Sheba came out of the doghouse.

Burl lassoed up Sheba to the dog harness and headed out.

They walked around the block that Burl knew of since childhood took about twenty minutes.

Back home, Burl, with Sheba in tow, went into the kitchen.

"Hey, Mom, can I help you with anything?"

"Sure, if you could just set the table, that'd be a great help."

"You got it, Mom," he responded.

A few moments later, the table was all set.

"Table's set, Mom. Can I help with anything else?"

"No, I think that's about all for now. If you could please call your father up for breakfast, that'd be great. Oh, if you could please pour the orange juice, we'll be all set."

Burl proceeded to the top of the steps leading down to the woodshop.

"Pops, time for breakfast."

"Be right up, Burl," he replied.

"Alrighty, Mom, Pop's on his way up now."

"Great. Could you please grab the dishes from the cupboard? Oh, and set the silverware and pour the orange juice."

"Sure, Mom."

Moments later, all was set for breakfast.

"Man, I'm hungry as hell."

"Same," replied Big John.

"Where's your father, Burl?"

"He's coming up right now."

"Great."

"When do you work next, son?"

"Tonight."

"Good. Your two sisters will be working there also. How's Audrey doing?"

"Great since the last time I spoke to her."

"Well, you hang onto that gal. She's the best woman I've ever met."

"Tell me something I don't already know."

"Just have to remind you now and then," Charlotte replied.

Pops then entered the kitchen. "Breakfast ready?" he asked.

"Yup, ready and waiting," Charlotte replied.

"Then let's chow down," said Big John.

At that, they all headed out to the dining room table.

"You serve up first," Charlotte said to Burl.

"Mom, this quiche looks fabulous."

"Hope it tastes as good as it looks. Could you please pass me the orange juice, Burl?"

"Sure, Mom, here you go."

"Oh dear, I forgot the coffee. Could you please get that for us, son?" Charlotte asked.

"Sure thing, Mom." Burl disappeared for a moment and came back with the coffee cups in hand along with a pot of coffee. "Here you go, Mom."

"Thank you, Burl."

"Son, could you please pass me the orange juice?" Big John said.

"No problem, Pops."

"Thanks."

"How do you like working at the Fish House, Burl?" Charlotte asked.

"I think that it's great, Mom. I get to see Audrey all the time. I'm working with two of my sisters, Buddy Bud Ange, and Big Chief. And I get to eat for free."

"Audrey's such a good woman," Charlotte replied.

"I know, Mom, such a great person."

"She's the cat's meow," replied his father.

"What're you guys up to today?"

"I'm gonna clean up the garden for next year's planting," said Big John.

"How about you, Mom?"

"I've got a bunch of laundry to do, and I'm gonna prepare for tonight's dinner."

"What've got in mind for dinner?" Burl asked.

"I'm thinking pepper steak, one of your favorites."

"Thanks, Mom, really appreciate it. But I'll probably eat at work."

"No problem, sweetheart," she replied.

"By the way, Pops, I wanna make a blanket chest for Audrey. Think I could do that?"

"Sure, what kind of wood are you thinking of making it out of?"

"I was thinking either cherry or walnut."

"Walnut's very expensive right now. I'd suggest going with cherry."

"How much does it cost?"

"It isn't cheap also. Going rate is $5.69 per board foot."

"I can afford that with the money I'm making at the Fish House. Know where I can get it?"

"Yeah, in fact, I do. You can get it from Stanford lumber supply. They're out of Hershey, Pennsylvania."

"When can you order it?"

"Right away, you can pay me with your next paycheck."

"What kind of finish you are thinking of putting on it?"

"I was thinking of rubbing it down with Danish oil."

"A really good choice. You won't have to worry about the mess a polyurethane makes."

"Cool," Burl replied.

"Hey, son," Big John said, "the Orioles are in the World Series today around 3:00 p.m. The first game starts against the Houston Astros.

"Need some help cleaning up the garden, Pops, until then?"

"Sure, I could really need some help," he replied.

The date was September 9, 1969, 12:00 p.m.

"Okay, son, you ready to help me out in the garden?"

"Sure thing, Pops."

At that, the two of them headed down to the garden.

"Whaddya want me to do first?" Burl inquires.

"Why don't you start by pulling up the corn stalks? That'd be a huge help."

"Sure thing, Pops." Burl then proceeded to do so.

The chore took Burl about half an hour to complete.

"What should I do with the corn stalks, Pops?"

"Just put 'em in the compost pile if you don't mind, son."

"Sure thing, Pops. What's next, Pops?"

"Why don't you pull the green beans and peas and add them to the compost pile?"

Burl proceeded to do so. This chore took Burl a full hour to complete. Time for lunch.

"Time for lunch, Pops. You wanna head up to the house?"

"Sure thing, Burl. I'll finish the rest later." The two then headed up to the house.

"Whaddya you two want for lunch? I have some leftover quiche if you'd like that."

"Sound good," Burl and Pops replied.

Charlotte brought in the quiche from the kitchen. "Dig in, fellas."

"Glady," said Burl.

The three of them ate voraciously.

"Hey, Pops, can we order the wood today for the blanket chest I wanna make for Audrey?"

"Certainly," Pops replied.

The three finished lunch around 1:30 p.m.

"Let's go order you wood now, son," Pops said.

"Sure thing," replied Burl.

"Now, what are the dimensions of your blanket chest?"

"About eighteen inches deep and about three feet long," Burl replied.

"Great. I think that you'll need about eighteen board feet of material. That'll cost you about $69. You got that much money?"

"Sure do, Pops."

"Great. Let's go ahead and order it." Pops dialed the number 1-800-369-6900.

"Thanks, Pops."

"No problem, son. Let's go upstairs and see what Mom's up to." Big John said.

"Hey, Mom, what's up?"

"Just doing laundry, dear."

"Can I help you out?"

"No thanks."

"Sure thing, Mom."

It was 3:30 p.m.

"Hey, Pops, how's it going?"

"Fine, son. How about you?"

"When's the wood supposed to arrive for my project?"

"Should be here no later than tomorrow, we can start on your project then."

"Great. What's on the agenda for the rest of today?"

"Well, I still have to do some work in the garden. Wanna help?"

"Sure thing, Pops," Burl replied.

They both headed down to the garden.

"Whaddya want me to do, Pops?"

"I need to spread the compost out over the garden and then till it under with the tiller. The tillers in the garage if you could please bring it down. Oh, and grab the wheelbarrow while you're at it."

"You got it, Pops," Burl replied. He then went up to the garage to retrieve the tiller and the wheelbarrow. Moments later, Burl returned to the garden. "Here you go, Pops."

"Great, son. Now fill up the wheelbarrow with the compost. We'll need about three loads."

"Sure thing," replied Burl.

He then proceeded to fill up the first load of compost.

"Now, son, start spreading it out evenly," Big John replied. "I'll do the tilling."

Burl proceeded to do so as instructed. All in all, the job took about three hours.

"Boys, time for lunch," Charlotte called out.

"Man, Pops, I really worked up a sweat."

"Me too," Big John replied. Then they both headed up to the house to eat lunch.

"Mom, lunch smells great," Burl said.

"Well, Burl, it's one of your favorites."

"Got that right, Mom," he replied.

"Burl, could you please get the ice tea and lemon from the refrigerator along with some ice and glasses."

"Sure thing, Mom," he replied. He then headed out to the kitchen to get the rice.

"So did you men get accomplished what you set out to do?" Charlotte asked.

"Yes, we did," Big John replied. "Worked up hell of a sweat. Well, it is summertime, you know. Anyone hear a weather forecast?"

"In fact, I did," Charlotte replied.

"Well, what was it, Mom?"

"Ninety-nine degrees, 69 percent relative humidity."

"No wonder we sweated so much, Pops."

"I know, but now I'm prepared for next summer's planting," Big John replied.

"We gonna go on vacation this year?" Burl asked.

"Yes, in fact, we are," Big John said.

"Where to?" Burl asked.

"Fenwick, Island."

"Cool. You gotta a place rented out?"

"Sure do," Charlotte said. "It's a really beautiful place, right on the water."

"How many bedrooms?" Burl asked.

"Six. Gotta be big enough to accommodate a family of ten people."

"Do they allow pets?" Burl asked.

"Yup, sure do," Big John said.

"Great, then we can take Sheba along."

"Cool."

"What breed is Sheba anyway?" Burl asked.

"Part Husky, part German shepherd," Big John replied.

"I really love Sheba. She's a great dog."

"She's a real sweetheart," Charlotte replied.

"Think we'll ever get a cat?" Burl asked.

"Actually, we were thinking we might," Big John replied.

"Know where we can get one, Pops?"

"Yes, there's a kennel on Route 28. Right next to Rabinol Engineering where I work."

"Cool. Have you checked them out, Pops?

"Not yet, you wanna go with me to pick one out, son?"

"Damn right, when can we go?"

"How about tomorrow, son? Mom's gotta go shopping at the co-op in Rockville. We can stop by there on the way home."

"Right on!" Burl replied.

"Great, then we'll do it."

"Whaddya got planned for tonight?" Burl asked.

Wanna watch the game with me?"

"Can't, Pops. I'll be at work."

"That's too bad."

"The O's gotta a chance of winning the pennant."

"Where're they playing?" Burl asked.

"Memorial stadium. They're playing the Yankees."

"Really? I thought it was the Red Sox."

"No, they got eliminated by the Blue Jays."

"Who's pitching?" replied Burl

"Jim Palmer," Big John replied.

"How about third base and the outfield?"

"Well, you got Brooks Robinson on third base and Frank Robinson in the outfield."

"Then that's a no-brainer, Pops. They should win easily," Burl said.

"Well, if Earl Weaver has his stuff together, I'd agree with you. But as they say, anything can happen on any given Sunday."

"Who's pitching for the Yanks?"

"It'll either be Jack Aker, Stan Bahnsen, Bill Burbank, John Cumberland, Al Downing, Steve Hamilton, Ken Johnson, or Mike Kekich."

"Know who's catching for the Yankees?" Burl asked.

"Either John Ellis or Frank Fernandez."

"Who's playing first base and center field?"

"Mickey Mantle of course," Big John replied.

"You know Mantle bats both ways and throws right-handed?" Big John said.

"Also, he slugged 536 home runs with a .298 batting average and 1,509 runs batted in. He was also a switch-hitter. From home to first base, he was clocked an incredible 2.9 seconds, and he could run the bases at an amazing 13 seconds."

"Damn, Pops, you know a hell of a lot about baseball. Who taught you all this stuff?"

"Believe it or not, I learned a lot of it off of baseball cards," he replied.

"Wow! I'm really impressed."

"Well, you can catch up with me if you start reading baseball cards."

"Do you know who hit the longest home run?"

"That I don't know."

CHAPTER 4

"Hey, Pops, think that I'm gonna take a quick nap before I go to work."

At that, Burl went upstairs to take his nap.

When lying down, he went into a deep sleep and started dreaming. While doing so, he dreamed about his family thinking about how lucky he was to have such a large one.

First, there was Jacquie (a.k.a. Jacklaun), a real estate appraiser. She was a really great woman. Burl loved the hell out of her. Then there was Andrea (a.k.a. Ange); she was a nurse and took very good care of him. Burl would later that he suffered from bipolar illness. Burl would later marry Audrey, the best woman he ever met with emerald-green eyes and full red lips. The two of them would later give birth to Andrew (a.k.a. Drew Beatz), who was an awesome music producer; he produced for Busy Bones and Pastor Troy. Ange was also a great woman; she married Franky and would take Burl to all his doctor's appointments of which there were many. Next in line was Burl, followed by Patricia (a.k.a. Buddy Bud), also a very good person who was married to Joe. Next in line was Timothy (a.k.a. Timmy), married to Christine. Both were fundamentalist Christians, which Burl loved since he was born and raised Catholic. Next, there was John, the Buddhist married to Marla, who would later die of cancer. Burl loved John (a.k.a. Little John) very much. Burl, at one point, was thinking of converting to Buddhism but decided Christianity was better suited for him. Finally, there was Melvin the Jew, who took care of all of Burl's finances, which was a good thing. Burl was fortunate in that Audrey left him an insurance policy amounting to about $3 million.

Finally, there was Big John and Charlotte, his mother. Big John would die of lung cancer, and Charlotte would die of stomach or esophageal cancer or some such shit. That completed Burl's ancestry.

Can't forget Susan and Jimmy Marple. They all played softball together. The first team that they played on was named the Fence Finders, a name coined by Burl. Then there was the Hills Angels, also named by Burl. The teams were moderately successful. They were first in the "A" league but usually got bumped down to the "B" league. They never won a championship no matter how hard they tried.

Almost forgot to mention Jeffrey (a.k.a. Big Chief), married to Janet, with three kids: Luke, Bridget, and Christopher. Big Chief was pretty cool in that Burl and he shared common interests. They both loved to read comics and build plastic airplanes, which they would hang from the ceiling, and they both loved to fish.

Burl also had a plethora of nieces and nephews.

Jacklaun had three: Carly (a.k.a. Carl), Austin (a.k.a. Aussie), and Travis (a.k.a. Trav). Big Chief had three, already mentioned. Burl, two, already mentioned. Ange, none. Buddy Bud, two. Lewis (a.k.a. Lew) with a beautiful gal named Emily (a.k.a. Em). Bryan with a wife, Shannon, and two great-grandchildren (Maxy and Dylan). Timmy and Christine (Jessie, Nate, and Danny). Little John (Lucy, Stephanie, and Zachary) with two great-grandchildren. Sydney (Rose and Martin), a transgender. And finally, Melvin, two kids (Jake and Shanna).

Regarding Burl, he grew up in Glen Hills, a subdivision of Rockville, Maryland. He first attended Beall Elementary School and was then transferred to St. Mary's Parochial School in Rockville. The first nun that taught him was Sister Boniface, a hard-ass bitch. Then it was Sister Martina who Burl really liked. Back then, they read the scholastic readers, but Burl wasn't a very good reader. Math, he sucked at—couldn't get subtraction, multiplication, or division despite the training from Big John, who was a self-taught engineer and mathematician. Burl became an altar boy at the tender age of twelve under the tutelage of Father John Silk, another hard-ass. Burl remembered the day when some parishioners were lined up along the rear wall of the church. Silk got so angry that he made them leave the church. Father Reddy was the monsignor at the time.

Burl attended St. Mary's up until the sixth grade, at which point he transferred to Robert Frost Junior High School through the seventh grade, at which point he was transferred to Thomas S. Wootton High School.

Burl fared well at Wootton, although he didn't do so well in geometry, taught by Mr. Distad. He excelled in history, taught by Mr. Evans. He did well in English, taught by Mr. Burtynsky, and did well in psychology, taught by Ms. Hayfitz. Tommy was in his class, and they both loved to check out her tight little ass.

Burl also took chemistry and biology, both of which he failed at miserably, ironic in that he later excelled in both was the fact that he was stoned half the time. It was customary to go over the hill by the tennis courts to smoke weed. He'd be accompanied by friends and sisters.

Burl was also smoking cigarettes at the time. Any brand, you name it: Marlboro, Salem's, even the less desirable Camels. The smoking area was just down the hall from the gymnasium. Burl eventually quit smoking when he was eighteen years old.

Burl and Tommy were best of friends; they did weed together long with Jim, Sam, and John (not Little John).

Burl remembered the time on Burl's eighteenth birthday when he and Tommy were canoeing on the C&O Canal just outside the District of Columbia. They were fishing, usually for catfish and smallmouth bass. Burl stood up on the canoe and tipped the canoe over, funny. Burl also got laid for the first time by Ginger Statts; this was before he met Audrey.

Burl also had other friends. Russell Rankin, Peter Bray, and Matty McMcain. Burl went to his prom for the first time with Casey Salon; he didn't get laid. Burl went to Wootton's prom with Lee

Cordon; once again he didn't get laid. But he did go to Audrey's prom at Church Hill High School and got laid.

Audrey's brother Ian would routinely catch Burl banging Audrey on her couch on Cranford Drive in Potomac, Maryland. Ian was the boy at the time before becoming a man named Burl. It all started with Sterling Nuts, which eventually morphed into Burl. Go figure.

Burl was screwing Audrey before her prom. Audrey's mother was Anne Burdick, who would later become a real bitch when they moved to their home in Germantown, Maryland. The damn cunt. She would come up from her room in the basement and barely give Burl an acknowledgment. The fucking whore, she paid for Audrey's education at Mount St. Mary's College with money that she acquired from probably from fucking Bin Lewis. Burl couldn't stand the bitch. Her one saving grace was that she would make up her bed in her room to allow Burl and Audrey to sleep together.

On one such occasion, Larkin McFee caught Burl and Audrey banging away in Audrey's room. Weird. She sat down on Audrey's bed, although they weren't screwing at that time at chatted as if nothing unusual was happening.

Burl had acquired a multitude of friends over the sixty-four years of his life. First, there was his best friend, Tom, who had two kids named Caleb and Evan He also befriended Tommy who had a brother Bill who was married to Barb. Burl also befriended Rob and Paul along with his sister Mary who was married to Alan. Then there was Kathy (a.k.a. Little Kadacky) who had a husband Mikey and a grandchild named Max. Next, there was Russell and Peter, followed by Rich, followed by Steve. Then there was Sam John Crowley and finally Jim and Kevin.

In terms of in-laws, there was Gwen and Bryan who had two children, Cameron and Amanda. Also included was Marla Slafgus.

Susie Jacobs and Joseph Acton (a.k.a. the Reverend), and Frank Eason married Ange; and Christine Kortum married Timmy, who had four kids: Jessie, Danny, Nate, and Emily.

Burl graduated from Wootton High School in 1976 and then moved on to Montgomery College in Rockville. Burl excelled while attending MC. He took algebra with Ange; and the three of them—Burl, Audrey, and Ange—took psychology with Mrs. Simons.

It was then that Burl started his education in earnest. He enrolled in Introduction to Chemistry along with Ange. Their instructor was Dr. Bob Coley who was an excellent instructor. He taught them how to balance chemical equations and stoichiometry. It was here that he learned of the two laws of the universe.

The first law of thermodynamics states that energy can neither be created nor destroyed, only moved from one place to another. The second law of thermodynamics states that the state of entropy and the entire universe, as an isolated system, will always increase over time. It also states that the changes in the entropy in the universe can never be negative.

There was no laboratory instruction during this course. After completing introductory chemistry, he then took inorganic chemistry taught by Dr. Bill Kenney. Burl didn't fare so well in this class but still managed to pull out a "C."

Burl then left the Rockville campus of Montgomery College and moved onto the MC campus in Germantown. Bob Coley was teaching organic chemistry at this point. Burl excelled in this class and easily pulled out an "A." He also took physics taught by Ernie Sherman; he excelled in this course as well.

Burl graduated from MC in the spring of 1978 fully stoked over his capabilities as a student. It was then that he realized that he had it in him to attain a high level of success as a college student.

He then applied to St. Mary's College in Southern Maryland. His good friend Jim McNesby and Tom Haynos's brother Dan attended SMC and had stellar accolades for the college. As such, Burl decided to attend the college if he was accepted.

He hung out at his parent's crib over the summer of 1976, waiting anxiously to see if he was accepted to SMC, which he didn't mind since he'd be able to see his main squeeze, Audrey.

On August 19 Burl got word that he was accepted to SMC. He was somewhat ambivalent in that he'd no longer be able to see his sweet love, Audrey, but figured what the hell. He thought, *I gotta move on with my life.*

Immediately after receiving his acceptance letter, he called Audrey. "Sweetheart, guess what?"

"What?" she replied.

"I got accepted to SMC. Whaddya think?"

"Oh, I'm so proud of you, my love, but I'm gonna miss you so very much."

"I'm gonna miss you too, sweetheart, but I promise you that I'll come home every two or three weeks."

"Well, I guess that's okay, but you promise?"

"Absolutely," Burl replied. "I'll still get to see you at the Fish House in the meantime over the weekends."

"That's true," said Audrey. "When you gonna leave?"

"As late as possible. I wanna see you as much as I can before I leave."

"Great. I was hoping you'd say that," she said.

"What is your plan, sweetheart?" Burl asked.

"I've applied to Mount St. Mary's College in Emmitsburg."

"What program are you looking at?" Burl asked.

"Business and finance," she replied.

"How's it looking?"

"Pretty good since I graduated from Churchill High School with a 4.0 GPA.

"Then I have all the confidence in the world that you'll get accepted."

"You know of anyone else that attends the Mount?" Burl asked.

"In fact, I do. Little Kadacky does."

"That's great, you'll have somebody to hang out with."

"I know, but I'd rather have you than Little Kadacky," she replied.

"Well, just remember, we'll be able to see each other over the weekends."

"I know my love."

"What do you have going on tonight?" Burl asked.

"Working at the restaurant," she replied. "How about you?"

"Same."

"Great, then we'll be able to see each other," Audrey replied.

"Need a ride?"

"In fact, I do. You wanna pick me up?"

"Love to," Burl replied. "What time?"

"Well, I have to be at the restaurant at 7:00 p.m."

"Good. I'll pick you up at 6:45 p.m."

"Great. I'll see you then, honey bunch," Audrey replied.

"Good see you then, my dear. Mom, is dinner almost ready for you and Pops?" Burl asked.

"Not even. I've been doing laundry all day and had to go to the grocery store," Charlotte replied.

"Where's Pops?"

"In the basement, where else?" she replied. "He's working on a bookshelf that he's building for us."

"I'm gonna say goodbye to him," Burl replied. "Hey, Pops, how's it going?"

"Great, son. Just working on the bookshelf," he replied.

"What are you making it out of?"

"Red oak," said Big John.

"What are you up to Burl?"

"Getting ready to go to go to work."

"Has Mom got dinner ready?" Big John asked.

"Naw, she's been doing laundry all day and had to go to the grocery store."

"Know what she's making for dinner?"

"I think pepper steak," Burl replied.

"How're you getting to work?"

"I'm driving. I gotta pick Audrey up in about a half hour."

"What car are you taking?" Big John asked.

"I was thinking the Corvair if that's okay.

"Sure, but you'll have to put some gas in it. It's almost on empty."

"What kind of gas you been putting into it?" Burl asked.

"High test."

"Wow. How much does that cost these days?"

"About $4.69 a gallon."

"Damn, that's expensive," Burl replied.

"I know, son. The oil embargo has really driven the price of fuel up. You sure you don't wanna take the station wagon?"

"Naw. How am I gonna impress Audrey by driving a station wagon?"

"Well, I don't think Audrey really cares."

"Sure, she does, Pops. She's a classy woman."

"If you say so."

"Gotta go, Pops. I'll catch you later."

"Goodbye, son. Have a good day at work, and make lots of money."

"Will do, Pops. Have a good day as well," Burl replied. "Mom, you know where my work uniform is?"

"Yes, it's up on your bed. I just finished folding it."

"Thanks, Mom."

Burl really didn't like the Fish House uniforms. The shirt was like the American flag—blue, white, and red stripes. Pants were navy-blue Dockers. What he thought could be worse.

He got dressed and headed out the door.

"Bye, Mom, I'm taking off."

"What time you gonna be home dear?"

"Probably kind of late. We usually go to a Chinese restaurant on the lower level of the shopping mall."

"Good. Just be careful."

"Will do, Mom." He then gave Charlotte a peck on the cheek and headed out. He got into the Corvair and cranked the engine. *Damn*, he thought, *this baby purrs like a kitten*. And off he was to pick up Audrey.

He wheeled into her driveway at six forty-five as promised. He knocked on the door to her house. "You ready, sweetheart?"

"Ready and waiting," she replied.

The drive to the Fish House took all about fifteen minutes, just in the nick of time for work.

Audrey wore her hostess outfit. It looked like a nurse's uniform except it wasn't white and had no headdress. Burl thought she looked cute nonetheless.

They entered the door to the restaurant.

"Catch you later, sweetheart," Burl said.

"Alright," she replied.

Burl then entered the kitchen.

Ange, Buddy Bud, and Patrice (a good friend of Buddy Buds) were hard at work.

"What's happening ladies?" Burl asked.

"Where you been Burl?" Ange asked.

"Just got here."

"Well, you're just in time. We have a lot of work to do."

"Where should I get started?"

"Need six bowls of hush puppies filled up," Ange replied.

"You got it, sis," Burl replied.

Dave Fields, the manager of the restaurant, entered the kitchen.

"Hey, Dave," Burl said.

"How's it going, Burl?"

"Pretty good. How 'bout you?"

"Not bad, but we've got a party of twelve coming in."

"Really."

"Yup, so you better get busting ass."

"Will do," Burl replied. Burl proceeded to the buffet line. "Hey, Joe, need six bowls of hush puppies."

"You got it," he replied.

At that point, Audrey entered the kitchen.

"Hey, guys, the party of twelve just arrived."

Patrice said, "Gotta get moving you all."

"Gotcha covered," Buddy Bud replied.

"Here're your hush puppies, Burl."

"Thanks, Joe."

Burl then loaded the six bowls of hush puppies onto his serving tray.

"Where do the hush puppies go?" Burl asked Patrice.

"Station 17," she replied.

"Alrighty then," Burl replied.

"Oh, and they need two pitchers of beer, six mugs."

"But there's twelve of them."

"Yeah, but half of them are kids who aren't allowed to drink."

"Gotcha," Burl replied. He stopped by the bar on the way to the table. Mike Blade was working the bar that night. "Hey, Mike, need two pitchers of beer, six mugs."

"You got it pal, anything else?"

"Not just yet, but they have six kids along, so I'll probably need soft drinks."

"Just tell me when, and I'll get 'em for you," he replied.

"Thanks, man," said Burl, and he was off to the table. Burl got to the table. "Good evening, folks. My name's Burl, and I'll be your server for the evening. Are you ready to order?"

A rotund man sitting at the head of the table responded, "Not just yet, Burl. We're still deciding. Do you have anything on special tonight?"

"In fact, we do. We have Louisiana frog legs and fried flounder."

"None of us like frog legs. Anything else?"

"We do have Alaskan crab legs and a variety of other things, however."

"How do the crab legs look?"

"Great. We just got a shipment in today."

"Cool."

"Can I get the kids anything to drink?"

"Sure, just bring us a pitcher of Pepsi."

"You got it, sir. Anything else?"

"Nope, that'll do it for now. We should be ready to order when you get back with the Pepsi," the rotund man replied.

Burl then headed back to the bar to retrieve the Pepsi. "Hey, Mike, need a pitcher of Pepsi, six glasses."

"Gotcha covered, my friend," he replied.

Several minutes later, Burl returned to the table. "You all decided what you'd like to eat?

"Sure have. I'd like the crab legs and flounder for the children, steamed shrimp for my wife, fried clams, and fried oysters for the rest of us."

"Sounds good. I'll get right on it," Burl replied and he was off to the kitchen.

He entered the kitchen to find Buddy Bud and Ange talking to Audrey. "Gals, what's up?"

"Just filling orders," Buddy Bud replied.

"Audrey, how're doing?" Burl asked.

"Just busy as shit," she replied.

"Well, it's Friday night. What would you expect?"

"I know, dear, but I didn't expect it to be this busy," she replied.

"Just hang in there, sweetheart," Burl replied.

"I know, but I can't wait to get out of here."

Barbie Hudson, the head waitress, entered the kitchen.

"Come on. guys, get to work," she said.

"Will do," they all replied.

At that, they all got busy to work.

Josie and Mike Prescott entered the kitchen.

"Hey, what's happening, Josie?" Burl asked.

"Not much, just busy as hell," she replied.

Mike Gilder then entered the kitchen along with Patrice.

"Hey, Mike," Buddy Bud asked, "how goes it?" Buddy Bud was particularly interested in that she had the hots for Mike.

"Pretty good," she replied. "How about you, Buddy Bud?"

"Pretty good, but it's busy as shit."

"I know, I can't believe it."

"Well, it is Friday night, you know."

Audrey then entered the kitchen again.

"Hey, Ange, you gotta party of four, station 3."

"Thanks, Audrey. I'll get right on it."

"And, Buddy Bud, you gotta party of six, station 4."

"Thanks, Audrey."

"No problem," she responded.

"And, Mike, you gotta party of three, station 7."

"Thanks, Audrey."

They all headed out of the kitchen to their respective positions.

Cynthia Rao, the assistant manager, entered the picture.

Damn, Burl thought to himself, *she's a beautiful woman.* She stood about five feet eleven inches, brown eyes, brown hair, and easily a 36 × 24 × 36. *I'd bang the shit out of her if I didn't already have Audrey*. "Hey, Cynthia," Burl replied, "how goes it?"

"Good, Burl. How 'bout you?"

"Pretty good, thanks for asking."

"Order up!" Joe said. The flounder, crab legs and steamed shrimp, oysters, and clam strips were ready to be served.

"Here, Burl, let me help you out," Cynthia said.

"Thanks, Cynthia, could really use the help."

"Surely, Burl," Cynthia said.

Great, Burl thought, *I can watch Cynthia's sweet little ass sway from side to side on the way to the table.*

"What station we going to?" she asked.

"Station 17," Burl replied.

"Have you served them hush puppies yet?" she replied.

"Oh hell, I almost forgot," Burl said.

"That's okay, Burl. You just serve the food, and I'll pick 'em up."

"Thanks, Cynthia."

"No problem," Cynthia responded. At that, they were off to station 17.

Several moments later, they both arrived at station 17.

"Sir, can we please have some hush puppies? We never got any," a youngster asked.

"Sure thing. I'll get them right away." Several minutes later, Cynthia returned with the hush puppies. "Here you go, folks."

"Ma'am, is our food almost ready?"

"Yes. Burl will get it for you shortly," she responded.

Burl headed back to the kitchen to retrieve the food. "Joe, Joe, is the food ready for the party of twelve?"

"So let me see, you had one order of crab legs, two orders of steamed shrimp and six orders of fried flounder, and an order of clam strips, is that right?"

"You got it, brother."

"Just give me about ten minutes and I'll have it ready for you."

Burl headed back to station 17. "Folks, food will be ready in about ten minutes. Can I get you anything before then?"

The rotund man replied, "Sure, Burl, we'd like another pitcher of beer and another pitcher of Pepsi."

"Anything else, sir?"

"Actually, yes. How 'bout another round of hush puppies, the kids really love 'em."

"Gotcha covered sir." At that, Burl was headed back to the kitchen.

"Order up!" Joe belts out.

"Here you go, Burl. Here's your order."

"Thanks, man."

Dave approached him.

"Need help serving the food?" He asked Burl.

"Yes. In fact, I could really use some help."

Ange came into the kitchen.

"Ange, could you please help out your brother serve up his order?"

"Sure thing," Ange replied.

"Ange, if you could please load up the serving trays, I'll get the drinks for the table."

"Anything for you, brother," she replied.

"Thanks so much, Ange."

Burl then headed back to the bar to pick up the beverages.

"Hey, Mike, need another pitcher of brew and another pitcher of Pepsi."

"You got it," he replied.

"Thank you, my friend."

A couple of minutes later, the beverage order was ready, and he returned to the table.

"Here you go, folks, Pepsi for the children and beer for the adults. Anything else I can get you?"

The rotund man replied, "No thank you, Burl. I think that we're all set."

At that point, he returned to the bar where he ran into Ricky High, another waiter.

"Hey, Ricky, what's happening?"

"Not much. Can't wait till the night's over. How 'bout you?"

"Same, man."

"What're doing after work?"

"Going down to the Chinese restaurant downstairs. You know Hunan Delight. It's the joint on the lower level of the shopping center. You wanna join us?"

"Sure, man, once I get out of this shithole. What time are you thinking?"

"Probably around ten thirty."

"Cool," replied Ricky.

At that, Burl headed back to the kitchen where he ran into Audrey. "Hey, sweetheart, how's it going?"

"Oh, I'm glad that you're here."

"How so?"

"Rich, Russell, Tommy, and Matty are here. They're waiting for you to serve them."

"What stations, my love?"

"Station 9," she replied.

Burl gave Audrey a slight peck on her cheek and thanked her. Burl approached station 9. "What's happening, fellas?"

"Just waiting to chow down on some food."

"Cool. What're you guys thinking?"

"Let's start with the fried flounder. It's the cheapest, isn't it?"

"Yup," replied Burl. It was customary for them to order the least expensive items on the menu and then move on to the more expensive crab legs. "What're guys want to drink?"

"How 'bout a pitcher of Budweiser in four frosty mugs."

"You guys gonna pay for this shit?"

"Hell no," replied Rich. "But we will give you a $40 tip. We'll all pitch in ten bucks."

"Cool," replied Burl. "I'll get right on it."

"Oh yeah, can you bring us some hush puppies?" asked Russell.

"Sure thing, man," Burl replied, and he then headed back to the kitchen. "Joe, need four bowls of hush puppies."

"Hey, man, you got any weed?"

"Sure do, my friend. We'll toke up on the loading dock after work."

"What kinda weed is it?"

"Only the best, I gotta three-finger lid of Colombian red."

"Cool," replied Joe. "I'll get your hush puppies right away."

"Thanks, man," Burl replied. He then headed to the bar to pick up the Bud.

"Hey, Mike, need a pitcher of Bud with four frosty mugs.

"Gotcha covered," he replied.

A couple of minutes later, Burl loaded the brew and mugs onto his circular serving tray. He then approached his friend's table.

"Here you go, fellas."

"Thanks, Burl," Tommy replied. "Believe me we'll make it worth your while."

"Cool," replied Burl. At that point, he headed back to the kitchen.

Patrice, Ange, Buddy Bud, and Audrey were all huddled back in the corner of the kitchen.

"What's happening ladies?" Burl asked.

"Were just discussing what we'll do after work," replied Buddy Bud.

"I was telling Ricky that we'd head down to Hunan Delight after work, what'd you guys think?"

"I'm down for that," replied Audrey. "You all into that?"

"Sure thing," replied Ange and Buddy Bud.

"Great, then we have a date," replied Burl. "Man, I don't know about you, guys, but I'm tired as shit."

"We are too," replied Patrice.

"Order up!" Joe blurts out.

"Gotta get back to work, ladies," said Burl.

"Go right ahead," replied Ange.

Burl loaded up his tray with hush puppies and fried flounder and approached station 9.

"Here you go, guys. Anything else I can get you?"

"Yeah, how 'bout them crab legs?" asked Tommy.

"They're coming, but I gotta be cool about it. Barbie the head waitress is keeping a close eye on what I'm bringing you guys."

"How 'bout another pitcher of Bud?" asked Rich.

"Man, you guys are gonna get me in trouble."

"Alright, alright, we'll cool it," said Russell.

"What're you guys into after I get off?" asked Burl. "I'm gonna toke up with one of the cooks on the loading dock after work and then head down to the Hunan Delight with Audrey and some of the other waitresses. You guys wanna join us?"

"Sure," they all replied.

"What kind of weed do you have?" asked Tommy.

"Some good shit, Colombian red. I got it from Kevin McNesby."

"You can count us all in," replied Russell.

"What time are you getting off work?" asked Matty.

"Probably around 10:00 p.m.," replied Burl. "Hopefully Hunan Delight will still be open."

"Should be," replied Tommy. "I don't think they close till 11:00 p.m.

"Cool," replied Burl. "You guys gonna join is at Hunan Delight?" asked Burl.

"Who's coming?" asked Tommy.

"A shitload of people," replied Burl. "Ange, Patrice, Buddy Bud, Jim and Josie Prescot, Ricky High, Mike Blade, Mike Gilder, Audrey, Joe the line cook, and you guys."

"Dude, you can count us in," replied Rich.

"Gotta get back to work, dudes," replied Burl.

"Were we gonna meet you?" asked Tommy.

"On the loading dock."

"Cool," replied Matty. At that point, Burl headed back into the kitchen.

Barbie was belting out orders. "You all can't leave until you fold silverware," she said.

Big Chief, who also worked there as a dishwasher, brought out the silverware. "Here you go, guys," he said.

"Damn, I hate folding silverware and Barbie as well," said Burl.

"You got that right," replied Patrice. They all agreed with her.

"Is Chief gonna join us?" asked Josie.

"Naw, he's not of drinking age," replied Ange.

"Shit, that's too bad.' Replied Jim.

They all finished up around nine thirty.

Joe approached Burl.

"Burl, you ready to toke up?"

"Damn right, dude. My friends Russell, Tommy, Rich, and Matty are gonna join us if you don't mind."

"Don't mind at all so long as you have enough weed," replied Joe.

"Yeah, I gotta three-finger lid," replied Burl

"Cool," replied Joe. "We gotta be careful though, we don't want Barbie or Dave to bust us."

"No worries," replied Burl. "I told Big Chief to be on the lookout for us if any of management comes our way."

"Cool," replied Joe.

At that point, Joe and Burl headed out to the loading dock where Russell, Tommy, Rich, and Matty were all waiting in anticipation.

"You got papers?" Burl asked Joe.

"Sure do, my friend," Joe replied. "You want me to roll a joint?" asked Joe.

"Yeah, roll one up," replied Burl.

Joe then does the honors. He rolls up a funnel-shaped European joint.

"Spark that sucker up," said Tommy.

Joe proceeded to do so with his Zippo lighter and took in a huge toke and then blew out the smoke.

"Man, this is some really good shit," said Joe.

"I told you only the best," replied Burl. "Pass it along," said Rich.

Joe then proceeded to do so.

Rich then took a big hit on the joint, held it in for a couple of seconds, and then blew out the smoke.

"Man, this really is some good shit."

"Told you so," said Burl.

"Pass that along," said Tommy. Rich proceeded to do so.

The joint then got passed along to all the rest of them.

Chief then came out to the loading dock.

"Quick, you guys gotta split, Dave's on his way out here.

They all then headed down to the Hunan Delight Chinese restaurant, the whole bunch of them. Upon entering the restaurant, they were approached by a hostess. "Good evening. How may I help you?"

"Party of fifteen," replied Burl.

"Oh my, did you make a reservation? We usually need advanced notice for such a large party."

Ange then joined the conversation. "Ma'am, with all due respect, we've been here many times with a party so large that we never had any problems getting served."

"Let me get the manager. I'll be right back."

A few moments later, the manager approached them. He was small in stature; very skinny; black hair cropped close to his head; and wearing a black Nehru jacket, white shirt, and black bow tie.

"Hello, my name's Yung Lee. Now, how may I help you?"

"Mr. Lee, we have a party of fifteen and need to be seated right away," said Ange

"Well, you need to make reservations for a party that large," he responded.

"I know that we've already been through this with your hostess. As you may or may not know, we're loyal regular customers here."

"I'll see what I can do. In that case, we may be able to seat you," Lee replied.

"Great. We'll wait," replied Ange.

He then entered the kitchen and returned moments later with the hostess and two busboys in tow.

"Alright, we can seat you, but it'll take a few minutes, we have to put some tables together." Mr. Lee said.

"Cool," replied Burl. "We'll wait.

Burl then turned toward Tommy.

"Dude, I don't know about you, but I'm stoned as shit."

"Fucking 'A,' dude. I am also," he replied.

"Are my eyes bloodshot?" Tommy asked.

"Yeah man, there're red as shit."

"Got any VISINE?" he asked Burl.

"Always man, go into the bathroom and put a few drops in each eye."

"Will do buddy, you're a life saver."

"No problem my friend."

Audrey then approached Burl.

"Where's Tommy going?" she asked.

"Going to the bathroom to do some VISINE."

"Wow! Is he really that stoned?"

"You better believe it. That weed's good as shit."

"When can I do some?" she asked Burl.

"How 'bout after work?"

"Sure, that'll work," he replied.

"Where'd you want to go dear?"

"I was thinking your house after work if that's okay."

"Sure is, but Ian's gonna be at home along with my mom."

"I guess that means we can't screw," Burl said.

"Sure we can, we just can't do it at my house."

"Where can we go then?" Burl asked.

"We can go to the field at Izaak Walton league off of Travilah Road in Potomac."

"Cool. I miss you so much, sweetheart."

"Same," she replied.

Finally, the waitress approached the large crowd after the bus-boys had put the tables together.

"Right this way," she spoke. The group then followed her to the table which would easily seat sixteen people, more than enough.

"Please have a seat," she spoke.

They all took a seat at the table with Burl at the head of the table.

"Now, can I get you all something to drink?"

"How about a round of mai tais for the entire table."

"You got it, sir."

"By the way, what's your name?" Burl asked

"Sun Yung Lee. I'm the manager's daughter."

"Cool," responded Burl.

"I'll be with you all in a few minutes to take your order," she spoke.

At that point, she was off to the kitchen.

"Whaddya in the mood for sweetheart?" Burl asked Audrey.

"I'm thinking General Tso's chicken. How 'bout you?"

"I'm thinking an order of spring rolls, egg drop soup, and sweet and sour pork."

"You want an appetizer?" Burl asked Audrey.

"Think I'll have an order of egg rolls and hot and sour soup."

"Sounds good to me my love," Burl replied.

The decor was typical Chinese—a statue of Buddha in the corner, an orchid at every table, and a silkscreen partition flanking the entrance.

"What are your plans moving forward?" Burl asked Audrey.

"Going to Montgomery College with you and Ange."

"Whaddya thinking of majoring in?" Burl asked.

"Business and finance. How 'bout you?"

"I'm thinking about biology even though I really sucked at it while attending Wootton."

CHAPTER 5

A few minutes later, Sun Yung returned to the table with the mai tais.

"Here you go folks, mai tais for everyone."

"Thanks, Sun Yung," replied Burl.

"Your quite welcome," she responded. She then took the order for the rest of the table.

"Audrey, now's a good time for us to smoke some weed, you wanna go outside?"

"Sure, let's do it," she replied.

They both left the table and proceeded to the back of the restaurant. Burl then pulled out a pack of papers and rolled a joint.

"Spark it up, sweetheart," Burl told Audrey.

"Sure thing, dear," she replied as she pulled out her Bic lighter.

She then sparked up the joint and took a huge toke and held it in for a few seconds and then blew the smoke out.

"Oh, Burl, this is some really good weed."

"I know sweetheart, I got it from Kevin."

"Think you could get me a baggie for me and Betsy?"

"Sure, but it's gonna cost you a pretty penny," Burl replied.

"Oh yeah, how much?"

"It's $69."

"That's not so bad dear, go for it," said Audrey. "Who're you getting it from?"

"Kevin, yeah, he sells some really good shit," she spoke.

"What are you into after work?" Audrey asked.

"Thinking of going home with you if that's alright."

"Now, you really don't have to ask, you're always invited to my house."

"Thanks, sweetheart. Think we can make love at your crib?"

"Are you kidding? Of course we can," Audrey replied.

"Great, 'cause I'm horny as shit," Burl replied.

"Same."

"Good, then let's get the show on the road."

They all finished eating around 9:30 p.m.

"Let's get the hell out of here," Burl told Audrey.

"Damn right, I can't wait to get home," she replied.

At that, the two of them headed out to the Corvair.

It was a beautiful summer night; not a cloud in the skies, and the sun was shining brightly.

"Hey, Audrey, why don't we pick up some beer?"

"Sure thing, what kind do you want?" she asked.

"How 'bout a six-pack of Schlitz," Burl replied.

"You got it dear, where should we go to get it?"

"Let's go to Belby's on the pike."

"Sure thing," she replied.

At that, the two of them were off to Belby's.

Burl went inside to order the beer.

A skinny fella was working the counter.

"Yes, sir. How may I help you?" he asked.

"Need a six-pack of Schlitz."

"Anything else?" Skinny replied.

"Yeah, let me get a couple of those giant Slim Jim's behind the counter."

Burl then headed out of the store and back into the car.

"Here you go sweetheart, a six of Schlitz and two giant Slim Jim's."

"Thank you, dear," she spoke. "Now, onto my house."

"Anything you say, my love." And off they were.

They arrived at Audrey's home at around 10:00 p.m. No one was home.

"Great!" Audrey said. "No one is here.

"Good," said Burl. "We have the house all to ourselves which means we can screw our brains out."

"Let's go into my bedroom," Audrey said. "What do you say we take these greasy clothes off?"

"Amen to that," said Burl.

They both remove their clothes.

"Man, my shirt is greasy as shit," Burl said.

"Let me put them in the wash," said Audrey.

"Go right ahead, sweetheart."

Audrey then went down into the basement to put Burl's shirt into the wash and returned a few minutes later.

"Alright, dear, take your clothes off," she said.

"Gladly, sweetheart," Burl replied. He then removed his clothing.

"Now, I'm gonna jump your bones," Audrey said.

"Ready and waiting, sweetheart," replied Burl.

The two screwed for a full hour.

"Sweetheart, that was unbelievable," Burl said.

"I feel the same way, dear. Now, what do you want to do?"

"Why don't we watch some tube?"

"Sounds good to me. What's on?"

"Let's watch something funny. I think *Saturday Night Live* is on."

"Sounds good to me," Burl replied. "What channel's it on?"

"I think NBC channel 4.

Burl changed the channel to channel 4.

"Here you go, sweetheart. It's on."

"Who's the guest on the show tonight?" Audrey asked.

"Alec Baldwin."

"Do you like him?"

"Naw, I think he's all washed up."

"Me too. Let's watch something else."

"Any ideas?"

"Try channel 69. I think *Nature*'s on. Supposed to be a special on sharks."

Burl changed to channel 69.

Sure enough, the shark special was on.

"Sweetheart, whaddya say we go on vacation soon?"

"Where'd you want to go?" Burl asked.

"How 'bout Ocean City?"

"Sounds good to me. What date do you want to go on?"

"How 'bout on our birthdays, the twenty-fifth and nineteenth of September?"

"That'd be great."

"Then it's a deal."

"Where's your mom and Ian at?"

"I think the Lewis's. You know Mom. She always wants to fuck Bin."

"Yeah, for that, you'd have to remove the cobwebs."

"Burl, you shouldn't talk about my mother like that."

"I know, but I think your mother is such a bitch."

"Bitch or not, I'd prefer it if you wouldn't talk about her like that."

"Alright, alright, I'll chill out."

"Good."

At that, they both retire to Audrey's bedroom for a good night's sleep. They woke up the next morning around 9:00 a.m.

"Morning, my love. How'd you sleep?" Burl asked.

"Great. How 'bout you."

"Like a baby."

"Whaddya have in store for today?" Burl asked.

"Gotta go to MC and register for my classes. How 'bout you?" Audrey asked.

"Same."

"Good, then we can go together."

"Fine by me," replied Burl.

"What classes are you signing up for?"

"Economics, algebra, psychology, and business and finance," replied Audrey. "How 'bout you?"

"Introduction to Chemistry, biology, human anatomy, and physiology."

"Cool."

"Wow! That's a heavy schedule, think you're up for it?"

"Gotta be. I'll be taking organic chemistry next year," Burl replied.

"Well, I just don't want you to get burned out."

"Don't you worry. I can handle it, sweetheart."

"Okay, if you're sure."

"Sure as sure can be," Burl replied.

CHAPTER 6

The next day the woke up at around 9:30 a.m.

"Morning, sweetheart.

"Good morning, my love," said Audrey. "What's up for today?"

"I gotta return the Corvair to my folks.

"How we gonna get to MC?" Audrey asked.

"We'll take the Blue Cloud," he responded. The Blue Cloud was a VW Beetle Burl's brother Little John had given him.

"Oh, I really love the Blue Cloud. It's such a cute little car."

"I know," said Burl

They arrived at Burl's parents' house on Valley Drive around ten thirty to return the Corvair.

They then entered the house.

"Mom, Pops, I'm home."

Burl's mom entered the room.

"Oh, hello, Audrey. Hello, Burl. What're you two up to today?"

"We gotta register for our classes at MC.

"You two want some breakfast before you head out?" asked Charlotte

"Sure, Mom. Whatcha got?"

"How 'bout scrambled eggs with grits and sausage?" replied Burl.

"Is that okay with you, Audrey?"

"Sure."

"Alrighty then, I'll get right on it," Mom replied.

Pops then entered the kitchen.

"Morning Burl, morning Audrey. Whatcha two got going for today?"

"We gotta register for our classes today," said Burl.

"That's great. What are you majoring in Audrey?"

"Business and finance," she replied.

"Really good choice, Audrey," Pops replied.

"Son, I know that you want to major in biology. What classes are you registering for?"

"Introduction to Chemistry, human anatomy and physiology, freshman biology, and physics.

"That's my boy, a chip off the old block. What car you taking?"

"The Blue Cloud."

"Good. How's the Corvair running?"

"Pretty good, but I think it may need new brakes."

"Why do you say that, son?"

"I don't know, they just seem a little squishy when you hit the brake pedal."

"Hmm, I'll have to take it to the mechanic to have a look at them. How's the Blue Cloud running?"

"Great. I wanna put a two-barrel carburetor on it."

"Where're you gonna get it from?"

"Grainger," Burl responded.

"A really good choice, they make excellent carburetors."

"Yeah, that's what Little John told me."

"Burl, you mind taking Sheba for a walk?"

"Sure thing, Pops. Audrey, you wanna go with me?"

"Yeah, sure."

At that, the two headed out to the doghouse to get Sheba.

"Come on, girl, let's go for a walk," Burl said.

Sheba wags her tail excitedly and barks loudly.

Burl harnesses her up.

"She's such a good dog, Burl."

"Yeah, I know, she's gotta be the smartest dog I've ever met.

I agree," said Audrey.

"Where you wanna walk her to?" asked Audrey.

"Just around the block. You wanna take the leash?"

"Sure thing," Audrey replied.

Audrey took the leash up Valley Drive, right on Overlea, right on Glen Road, right on Cleveland, and right on Valley Drive. Finally, back home.

"Nice walk sweetheart," Burl said.

"Really was, I'm outa breath," Audrey replied.

"So am I."

"Ready to head out to MC?"

"Sure thing, but I have to get changed, can you take me back to my house?"

"Yup," Burl replied.

"Good, then let's hit the road."

At that, they were off to the races in the Blue Cloud.

They arrived at Audrey's house at around 10:00 a.m.

"Let's go inside so I can get changed."

"Sure thing, sweetheart," Burl replied.

Audrey then changed into a pair of blue denim, a polo shirt, and a pair of white Chuck Taylor.

"Wow! You really look great sweetheart, especially with the Chuck Taylor."

"You really like 'em, do ya?"

"Yeah, I gotta pair of black high tops. Ready to hit the road?" Burl asked.

"Yup."

Burl then fired up the Blue Cloud. They then cruised down Falls Road and onto Mannakee Street and into the MC parking lot, lot 3.

"Let's go," said Burl.

"What building we supposed to go to?" Audrey asked.

"Administration."

"Cool. Let's go."

They entered the door to the administration building.

"Hello my friend," said Burl. Can you please tell me where registration is?"

"Sure thing. It's on the third floor, room 69."

"Thanks, man."

"No problem," the young man replied.

Burl and Audrey headed up to the third floor and entered room 69.

"Good morning. How may I help you?"

"We're here to register for classes," said Audrey.

"Well, you've come to the right place," the woman replied. "Now, what classes would you like to register for?"

Burl took over the conversation.

"I'd like to register for Introduction to Chemistry, Algebra II, physics, biology, and psychology."

"Alrighty, and how 'bout you, miss?"

"Business and finance, psychology, and Algebra II."

"Great. Please follow me," the woman said.

"By the way, what's your name Miss?"

"I'm Ms. Miller, and what're your names?"

"My name's Burl and this is my girlfriend, Audrey."

"Pleased to meet you two. Now, you must first fill out an application," Ms. Miller replied.

"Cool," Burl responded.

The application had the usual shit on it—name, address, phone number, and Social Security number.

"Wow! You two are lucky. Algebra II only has two more slots open. You're okay with psychology, plenty of room left."

"Now, Burl, what other classes did you want to take?"

"Introduction to Chemistry and physics and psychology."

"Alright, looks like you're all set." Ms. Miller replied. "Your first class is psychology."

"What building is that in?" Inquires Burl.

"That'd be building 69."

"Great. We're on our way," replied Audrey.

The two set off for building 69.

"Isn't it great Audrey, we're in all the same classes."

"I agree."

Coincidentally, psychology was being held in room 69.

They then entered the classroom.

"Now, any questions before we get started?"

Audrey raised her hand.

"Ms. Simons, what topics will we be covering?"

"A really good question."

"We'll be covering bipolar illness, schizophrenia, and obsessive-compulsive behavior."

Another girl raised her hand.

"Yes, ma'am."

"How will be graded?" she asked.

"Well, 10 percent of your grade will be on class participation, 40 percent on quizzes and tests, and 50 percent on papers."

"How long are the papers supposed to be?" she asked.

"Well, quite a lot, twenty pages at a bare minimum, extra credit for anything beyond that including bibliography."

"Okay, thank you."

"Anymore question?" Ms. Simons asked.

No one raised their hands.

"Alright then, let's get started."

"First, I'd like to get started with bipolar illness. Anyone know the symptoms of this illness?"

Burl, who had a subscription to *Psychology Today*, raised his hand.

"Isn't it characterized by high libido, run-on speech, and excessive spending?"

"Yes, that's right, and what's your name sir?"

"Name's Burl."

"That reminds me, let's arrange our seats in a circle and have each of you introduce yourselves."

Everyone went around the room and introduced themselves.

The class lasted for a full forty-five minutes.

"Now, before you leave, your first assignment will be to start a paper on bipolar illness. Remember the criteria, twenty pages at a bare minimum and detailed bibliography. Class dismissed."

Audrey and Burl headed out of the room.

"Damn, a twenty-page paper. Where the hell are we supposed to find information on bipolar illness?" Burl said.

"I've got a subscription to *Psychology Today*. We can probably find the information there."

"Cool but we better get on it right away."

Their next class was Algebra II in the science building, room 369.

They then entered the classroom.

"Good morning, class. My name's Mr. Squires. I'll be your instructor for this semester. We'll be studying many mathematical concepts. We'll cover binomial equations, polynomial equations, and trinomial equations. Do any of this sound familiar?" he asked.

I guy wearing Coke bottle glasses, slick-backed hair, and a pair of penny loafers raised his hand. The dude looked like Poindexter.

"Yes, sir, I know all of 'em," he replied. "I learned them in freshman algebra in high school."

"And what, may I ask, is your name?"

"Name's Earl. Earl Jackson, sir."

"Very good, Earl," Squire's replied. "Now, anyone else? Great, then let's get started."

Poindexter raised his hand.

"Yes, Earl, what do you think?" Squires asked him.

"Well, to balance a polynomial equation, you need to find out what the square root of the variable is."

"Right you are. What's next?"

"Then you need to figure out what the factorial is of the variable."

"Right again. Anything else?"

"No, I think that about does it."

"Anyone else?"

Burl raised his hand. "I think you need to plot the answer on the X and Y axis on graph paper," he replied.

"Correct, that's right."

The class was over in about an hour. Burl was off to biology class.

Upon entering the room, the instructor introduced herself, "Hello, class, my name's Ms. Alberts. I'll be your biology instructor for the rest of the semester."

"Now, why don't we start by introducing yourselves to the rest of the class."

Introductions go around the room.

"Great. Let's get started."

"First, we're gonna talk about mitosis. Anyone have any ideas?'

Burl raised his hand.

"First, there's prophase where the chromosomes line up. Then there's telophase followed by anaphase. Then there's DNA replication where the telomeres guide the chromosomes into position for replication."

"Very good, Burl. Anyone else have something to offer?"

No one else raised their hands.

"Great. Class dismissed."

Burl's next class was Introduction to Chemistry.

Burl entered the classroom.

"Hello, ladies and gentlemen, my name's Bob Coley. And I'll be your instructor for the semester. Anyone have any ideas as to what chemistry is about?"

Some nerd raised his hand.

"Well, I think it's about isotopes, Avogadro's number, molecular mass and number, protons, electrons, and neutrons."

"Very good. Did you take chemistry in high school?"

"Yes, I did in fact, but I gained most of my knowledge by reading books."

"Great. Anyone else have something to offer?"

Burl raised his hand.

"What's your name, sir?"

"Burl."

"Okay, Burl, let's have it."

"Well, I think chemistry is about balancing chemical equations and stoichiometry."

"Right you are," Coley replied.

"Anyone else?"

No one raised their hand.

"Alright then, class dismissed."

Great, the day's finally over, Burl thought. *Now, I gotta find Audrey.*

Burl figured she was probably in the library doing some homework. He went to room 369 on the third floor and found her working diligently on some schoolwork in one of the cubicles.

"Hello, sweetheart. How're doing?"

"Not so good, Burl."

"How so?"

"I'm working on some accounting homework and it's hard as shit."

"Just hang in there. You'll get it," said Burl.

"I really hope so," she replied.

"Let's head out now," said Burl.

"You got it, I'm hungry as hell."

"Where you wanna go?"

"I was thinking Hash Brothers."

"Cool. Let's go," Burl replied.

It was customary for them to go to this restaurant after school.

"Where's the Blue Cloud parked?" Audrey asked.

"Space 69 in parking lot three."

"Good. Let's get out of here," said Burl.

They found the Blue Cloud parked in the designated parking space and climbed into the car. The car had leather bucket seats and a leather steering wheel and a dual carburetor—a nice ride.

It only took fifteen minutes to drive from the college to the restaurant. They then entered the restaurant.

They meet a hostess in the foyer. "How may I help you?" she asked.

"Need a table for two," Burl replied.

"Right this way," the hostess replied. Her name was Sheila as indicated on her name tag.

She seated them at a two-top table.

"Here you go folks, the waitress will be right with you as she sets down two menus.

"What do you want to eat?" Burl asked Audrey.

"Think I'll go with the BBQ sandwich with a side of fries. How 'bout you?" said Audrey.

"Think I'll go with the pot roast on wheat bread and gravy with a side of coleslaw."

"What do you want to drink?" asked Burl.

"I think I'll go with a Coca-Cola. How about you?"

"Same," Audrey replied.

Sheila returned to the table.

"Now, what would you two lovebirds like to eat?"

"How about a BBQ sandwich with a side of fries for my gal, and a pot roast sandwich and gravy on wheat," replied Burl.

"What to drink?" Sheila replied.

"Two Coca-Colas if you don't mind," said Burl.

"You got it, honey," And off she was to the kitchen.

Burl stares intently into Audrey's beautiful eyes.

"I love you so much, sweetheart," Burl said.

"I love to too, my love," Audrey replied.

"Glad to hear it, sweetheart," Burl replied.

About a half hour later, Sheila returned with their food and drinks.

"Here you go folks, enjoy!"

And at that they did, eating voraciously. Starved as hell.

They finished eating about an hour later.

"What would you like to do later?" Audrey asked.

"I was thinking we'd go over to my house," said Burl. "I know my Mom and Pops would love to see you."

"That's cool," replied Audrey.

"Then it's a date," replied Burl.

It took about a half hour to get to Burl's parent's house. They pulled into the driveway and then entered the door leading to the back porch.

"Hey, Mom, hey, Pops, we're home." Sheba was also on the porch lying down next to Burl's father.

"What's happening guys?" Big John asked.

"Me and Audrey just got outa school," replied Burl.

"How'd it go?" Charlotte asked.

"Pretty good but it was a hell of a long day," said Burl.

"How 'bout you, Audrey? How'd it go with you?" asked Charlotte.

"Pretty much the same as Burl it was a long day."

"How so?" asked Big John.

"Introduction to Accounting was really tough. It took me about an hour to get through with it."

"Stick with it, dear," replied Charlotte. "You'll find a way to get through it, you're a really smart gal."

"Thanks, Mom, really appreciate it," replied Audrey.

"What's on the agenda for today?" Big John asked.

"I was thinking about taking Sheba for a stroll," replied Burl.

"Great," replied Burl's father. "She's long overdue for a walk."

"Okay, if Audrey stays for dinner?" Burl asked.

"Sure thing," replied Charlotte. "Would love to have her for dinner."

"What time are you thinking for dinner?" Burl asked.

"I was thinking about 6:30 p.m. Is that okay with you two?" replied Charlotte.

"Should be fine," replied Burl.

"Is that okay with you, Audrey?" asked Charlotte.

"Yes, that'll work just fine," replied Audrey.

"Great, then you gotta date," replied Charlotte.

'We're gonna take Sheba for a walk pronto," replied Burl.

"Alrighty then." And Burl and Audrey were off for the walk.

They then go out to the doghouse to leash up Sheba.

"Come on, girl, let's go for a walk," said Burl.

Sheba then wags her tail and barks excitedly.

"You wanna take the leash sweetheart?" asked Burl.

"Sure thing, dear," replied Audrey.

"Be sure to be back in time for dinner," Charlotte said.

"No problem, Mom," replied Burl.

CHAPTER 7

It was about 3:30 p.m. when Burl and Audrey returned from their walk. Pops and Charlotte were still sitting on the porch.

"Hey, Mom, hey, Pops, how's it going?

"Just doing the *New York Times* crossword puzzle. It's a really tough one."

Charlotte was knitting.

"Whatcha knitting, Mom?" Audrey asked.

"I'm knitting a sweater for Ange," Charlotte replied.

"What're making for dinner?" Burl asked.

"Pepper steak, one of your favorites. I'll get started on it around six thirty."

"Pops, you almost finished the crossword puzzle," Burl asked.

"Almost done son," he replied.

"What are you into after that?" Burl asked.

"I was thinking of watching some golf, the U.S. Open's on."

"Who's playing in it?" Burl asked his father.

"A really great lineup."

"Oh yeah, who's in the tournament?"

"Jack Nicklaus, Lee Trevino, Arnold Palmer, Chi Chi Rodriguez, and Gary Player."

"Wow! Let's watch it now," Burl said. "What channel is it on?"

"I think that it's on channel 9, CBS," Big John replied.

"Cool. I'll turn it on right now." Burl replied.

Burl entered the family room and turned the TV on.

"Pops, the tournament is on, come on in."

"Be right in." His father replied.

Audrey and Charlotte were still chilling out on the porch enjoying the beautiful September afternoon.

Pops entered the family room and sits down on his favorite leather wing-backed chair. Burl was sitting on the couch.

"Who's teeing up first?" Big John asked.

"I think it's Nicklaus," replied Burl.

"You know he shot a 69 in the Masters Tournament at Augusta International back in April."

"Wow! Nicklaus is quite a good golfer."

"What do you think his chances are that he wins the Open."

"Pretty good, but the rest of the field is pretty good as well," replied Big John.

"Yeah, but Trevino's been playing some really good golf lately," responded Burl.

"I know but Chi Chi's been playing some good golf lately, he also shot a 69 at the St. Andrew's links in the British Open.

Charlotte then entered the room with Audrey. "What's going on with you two?" Audrey asked.

"I think that I'm gonna continue knitting," replied Charlotte. "How 'bout you, Audrey?"

"Think that I gonna read the Sunday's paper. After that, I guess me and Mom will start dinner. What're you guys into?"

"We're gonna watch the US Open golf tournament. It should really be a good one, all the top players in the world will be playing," replied Burl.

"Great. We'll see you two around dinner time," replied Charlotte.

The tournament began with Gary Player teeing it up on hole number 1 and smoking the ball a full 369 yards down the fairway.

Next, Jack Nicklaus was up, and he slammed his drive 330 yards down the fairway.

Lee Trevino was up next and absolutely crushed the ball a full 369 yards down the fairway, just like Gary Player.

Finally, Chi Chi Rodriguez was up and duffed his shot; the ball only traveled 69 yards down the fairway, no mulligans here unfortunately.

Gary Player, the South African from Johannesburg, ended up winning the tournament with 269, 19 strokes under par.

"Man, what a tournament! Pops?" replied Burl.

"Sure was, son."

The tournament lasted a full three hours. Time to prepare dinner.

"Hey, Mom, need some help?" asked Burl.

"Sure, I could really use some help," she replied.

"Whaddya need help with, Mom?"

"If you could please set the table, that'd be helpful. Also, could you call Audrey in here?"

"Gotcha covered, Mom."

Audrey then entered the kitchen a few moments later. "Whatcha need help with Mom?" Audrey asked.

"Dear, if you could please cut up the green and red peppers and onion, that'd be great."

"You got it, Mom," she replied and proceeded to get the vegetables out of the refrigerator.

"John, could you please come in here right away?" Charlotte asked.

"What's up, dear?"

"I need you to cut up the sirloin."

"Sure thing. Where is it?"

"In the freezer, where else."

Big John went to the freezer to retrieve the sirloin steak. "Now, how'd like it cut up?" he asked.

"Silly, you act like you've never made pepper steak before."

"Alright, alright, just tell me how you'd like it cut up."

"Very thin slices, as thin as you can get," Charlotte replied.

"You got it, dear." Big John proceeded to cut up the sirloin.

"How are you coming along, Audrey?" Charlotte asked.

"Almost done, Mom."

"Where's Burl?"

"I'm right here, Mom. Whatcha need?"

"Could you please get me the soy sauce, minced garlic, ginger, sugar, and onion?"

"Sure thing. Anything else?"

"If you could please get the glasses, ice tea, and lemon that'd be great. Oh, and fill up the glasses with ice."

"You got it, Mom. He replied.

"Great. Dinner will be ready in about ten minutes."

"Can't wait," replied Burl.

"Me neither," said Audrey.

The two then march out to the back porch where Big John was sitting.

"Hey, Pops, how's it going?" Burl asked.

"Pretty good son, but I'll be damned if I can figure this crossword puzzle out."

"Pops, you gotta quit doing the crosswords, they're gonna drive you friggin' crazy."

"I know, but it doesn't hurt trying," he said.

"Pops, mind if Audrey and I go for a quick swim before dinner?"

Burl's father had put in an above-ground swimming pool, the cheap kind with corrugated metal walls and a small water pump.

"You gonna have enough time?"

"Should have. Mom says dinner won't be ready for about ten minutes."

"Okay, but don't be late. Mom's spent a lot of time preparing dinner," Big John said.

"No problem, Pops."

"Great. Ma and Audrey will go put on our swimsuits now."

The two then proceeded inside to put on their suits.

"Mom, Audrey and I are gonna go for a quick swim before dinner."

"That's fine, but please don't be late for dinner."

"I know, I know. That's what Pops just said."

The two then headed upstairs to Burl's room to change.

Big Chief, Burl's brother, was sitting on his bed.

"Hey, Chief, you mind leaving the room, Audrey and I have to get changed into our swimsuits."

"That's cool Burl, maybe I'll take Sheba for a walk."

"You better hurry, Mom's gonna have dinner ready shortly."

"Alright, I'll be sure to hurry." Chief left the room to take his dog for a walk.

Burl went to the highboy dresser to retrieve their swimsuits. He then opened the drawer second from the top.

"Here you go, sweetheart. Here's your swimsuit."

"Thanks, Burl."

"Aren't you gonna put your swimsuit on?"

"Sure, as soon as I can find the damn thing," he replied.

"Aah, here it is, right below the blue jeans."

"Well, then put it on," Audrey said.

Audrey then pulled off her clothing and proceeded to put on her thong bathing suit.

"Man Audrey, you have such a beautiful body."

"Thank you, dear. You really think so."

"I really know so," Burl replied.

Burl's pops got excited just looking at Audrey's body.

"Ready to go, sweetheart?"

"Sure am," Audrey replied.

"Sweetheart, your body just looks so fine."

"That may be so, ya think?"

At that point, they were off to the swimming pool.

"Okay, Pops, we're heading into the swimming pool."

"Sure you wanna go, the water's a bit chilly."

"Nothing we can't handle Pops." At that, Burl and Audrey were off for a swim.

Burl then dips his arm into the water.

"Man Audrey, Pops wasn't kidding, the water's cold as shit."

"Well, you can't say he didn't warn you."

"I know, I know, but let's hop in anyway." At that, they both climbed the ladder leading into the swimming pool. Burl was the first to go in.

Upon entering the water, he shimmers and shakes.

"Audrey, I think this water's so cold that my balls are shriveling up."

"Well, you can't let that happen."

"Here, you get in, sweetheart," Burl said. Audrey proceeded to jump into the swimming pool.

"Oh dear, the water is really cold, I think my nipples are shriveling up."

"I told you so sweetheart."

"Let's get out and help Mom with dinner."

"I second that motion," replied Burl.

The two then got out of the pool.

"Pops, you weren't kidding. The water's cold as hell."

"Don't say that I didn't warn you."

"Well, I guess you learn the hard way," Burl replied.

"We're gonna go help Mom with dinner," said Audrey.

"Go right ahead, Burl. I think dinner's almost ready." The two of them then headed into the kitchen.

"Hey, Mom, need some help?"

"Just gotta boil some rice, Audrey, would you mind doing that?"

"Sure thing, Mom. Where's the rice?"

"It's in the cupboard above the stove."

Audrey then proceeded to the cupboard.

"Burl, I can't reach the rice, could you please get it for me?"

"Sure thing, sweetheart." Burl grabbed the rice.

"Here you go, my love."

"Thanks, Burl."

"Here you go, Mom. Here's the rice, now what do I do?"

"Grab a pot from underneath the counter, fill it with two and a half cups of water, and then boil it on the stove."

"That's easy enough," replied Audrey.

Big Chief then entered the kitchen.

"Just walked Sheba." He said.

"How'd she do?" asked Burl.

"Great, but she did try to go for a swim in the Willis Pond."

"Well, did you let her?"

"Hell no, I ain't that stupid," replied Chief.

"Don't be so sensitive," responded Burl.

"Dinner's ready, you all," said Charlotte. "Come and get it."

They all headed to the dining room table in the family room.

"Mom, this looks delicious," replied Audrey.

"I hope so, I spent a lot of time preparing it." They all then take a seat at the table.

"Oh, I almost forgot the rice, would you mind getting it Chief?"

"Sure thing, Mom."

"Burl, could you please pass me the pepper steak?" asked Pops.

"Sure thing, Pops."

So, what are you two up to for the rest of the day?" asked Charlotte.

I wanna go fishing," said Burl.

"Oh yeah, where're you thinking about going to?" Big John asked.

"I was thinking about the Willis Pond," Burl replied.

"What kind of fish are they catching there?"

"Smallmouth bass, catfish, and sunfish. There's a big lunker catfish that I'd like to catch."

"What're gonna catch him on?"

"Probably chicken liver."

"You like to fish Audrey?" Charlotte asked.

"It's alright, but I never catch anything."

"Oh really."

"Yeah, my mom and father weren't much into fishing," she replied.

"I'm surprised with them living on the Florida coast and all."

"You'd think so, but they just weren't."

They finished eating dinner around 7:00 p.m.

"Hey, Pops, wanna go downstairs to your woodshop?"

"Sure thing. Let's go."

The two then headed down to the woodshop.

"Pops, I didn't want to talk about it in front of Audrey, but you think we can work on the blanket chest I had in mind for her?"

"Sure, what kind of wood do you have in mind?"

"I was thinking cherry."

"Good choice. It doesn't cup or warp much. What kind of finish are you thinking about?"

"I was thinking teak oil."

"A really good choice, it protects the wood much better then polyurethane."

"Cool, then let's get started," Burl replied.

"Wait son, I first have to order the lumber."

"Where're you gonna order it from?"

"Stanford Lumbers out of Everett, Pennsylvania."

"How long will that take?"

"Probably about two to three weeks."

"Aww Pops, I can't wait that long."

"Well, you're gonna have to son, I don't know what to tell you."

"If that's the best we can do, I guess that I'll have to wait."

"Please be patient, Burl. It'll be here before you know it. Let's go back upstairs."

"Hey, ladies, whatcha all into?" Burl asked.

"Just cleaning up after dinner," Audrey replied. "What are you and your father gonna do?"

"I don't quite know. Let me ask Pops."

"Hey, Pops, what're you into tonight?"

"Well, the Orioles are playing again, wanna watch the game with me?"

"Man, do I ever, they're in the race for the pennant."

"Great, then we have a date."

"Mom, Audrey, you wanna catch the O's game with me and Pops tonight?"

"Naw," Mom said. "I only watch baseball when the Milwaukee Brewers are in it."

"How 'bout you, Audrey? You wanna watch the game with us?"

"No, I'm gonna work on my accounting homework."

"Okay, be that as it may, you're gonna miss a really good ballgame."

"That's okay. Schoolwork is much more important."

"What time's the game on, Pops?"

"Seven oh five."

"I really never understood why five after seven is the first pitch. Why couldn't they just make it seven?"

"I know, son. It seems a little squiffy to me."

"You know who's pitching for the O's?"

"I think Jim Palmer."

"Who're they playing?"

"The Toronto Blue Jays."

"If that's the case, they should kick ass."

"Well, proof is in the taste of the pudding."

"Who's in the lineup for the Blue Jays, Pops?"

"I think Bo Bichette, shortstop. Vladimir Guerrero, first baseman. And Alex Manoah, pitcher."

"Wow! That's quite a lineup."

"You know much about Manoah's pitching statistics?"

"Yeah, he pitched a no-hitter against the Boston Red Sox just last week."

"Wow! He's really got his stuff together."

"You know how many he walked against the Red Sox?"

"Yeah, just three."

"You know what Manoah's ERA is?"

"It's 2.69. About the lowest in the American League."

"You know who won the MVP award in baseball during the 1978 season?"

"Yup, it was Jim Rice."

"Who are the other pitchers on the Blue Jays?"

"Tom Buskey who bats right-handed, Jim Clancy who bats right-handed, and Joe Coleman who also bats right-handed."

"You know who the outfielders are on the Blue Jays?"

"George Springer, Daulton Varsho, Kevin Kiermaier and Nathan Lukes."

"You know the catcher for the Jays?"

"There's actually two of em, Alejandro Kirk and Denny Jansen."

"Wow! You really know your stuff about the Jays. How'd you find all this out?"

"Just from the program," Big John replied.

Charlotte then entered the room. "You fellas want some popcorn for the game? I just bought some Orville Redenbachers."

"Sure thing, Mom."

"How about something to drink?"

"I'll have a Natty Bohemian," replied Big John.

"How about you, Burl?"

"I'll take a Coca-Cola if you have one."

"Sure do, dear."

"Can I get you boys anything else?"

"Think you've got it all covered," Big John replied.

"Great! I'll get right on it."

Audrey then entered the room.

"How's it going sweetheart?" Burl asked.

"Okay, but like I said, accounting is really tough."

"Sweetheart, you're really getting burned out on accounting. Why don't you switch to something else?"

"Good idea. Think I'll switch over to economics."

"Yeah, why don't you give that a shot sweetie?"

"I think Burl's right, Audrey," said Big John. "It's worth a try."

"I just hope that it's not as hard as accounting," she responded.

"Like I said, sweetheart, you're a really smart gal. You can surely handle it," said Burl.

"Thanks for the compliments," said Audrey.

"Sure thing, sweetheart."

Charlotte then entered the room with the popcorn and drinks.

"Here you go fellas, enjoy."

"Thanks, Mom," said Burl.

"No problem, dear."

Burl and Big John then proceeded to chow down on their food and drinks.

In the summer of 1978, Burl quit working at the Fish House and moved on to Lakewood Country Club, just down the street from his folk's house in Glen Hills.

It was here that he worked with Buddy Bud as a waitress, Big Chief who worked as a dish and pot washer, Amy Cohen who worked as a waitress, Peggy Hill who works as a secretary, Kathy McPherson, her brother Bunsy Lynn Oberson who worked as a waitress, and John Carroll who also worked as a dishwasher.

The maître d' that day was Smitty (who absolutely had the worst body odor), the general manager Bill Farmer, assistant manager Joe Marion, John Gardener who worked the mixed grill, Bryan Wilson who worked the bar in the main dining room, Louie the head chef, and finally Skeets who worked as the food and beverage manager. Skeets was a pervert. He'd come up to Burl and say, "How's my boy today?" and grope at his crotch.

He banged Lynn Oberson in the shower, the first shower sex that he'd ever had, until he met Audrey. He also banged Kathy McPherson later while attending St. Mary's College in Southern Maryland.

This was about the only time that Burl would be unfaithful and express his infidelity toward Audrey.

The first event that Burl waited on was a bar mitzvah. There was a plethora of Jews present, which was okay with Burl since he knew that Jesus Christ was a Jew and was raised Roman Catholic.

The dining room that day was crowded with Jewish people. On the menu was matzo ball soup being served along with gefilte fish and unleavened bread, which was generally served during Passover and the Eucharist if one were a Christian respectively. Beverage included Manischewitz wine.

Serving was nothing new to Burl or Buddy Bud for that matter since both had served table at the Fish House.

Smitty was the maître d' that day while Joe Marion was managing the kitchen and bar. John Gardner was managing the men's grill.

All hell broke loose during the ceremony. Little Jewish kids were throwing matzo balls around like untamed monkeys. Rabbi Silverstein was beside himself, thoroughly confused and not knowing what to do with the rowdy children.

Bill Farmer was saying, "Ladies and gentlemen, this isn't sensible!"

Unsensible or not, the crazy shit continued.

The bar mitzvah finally ended at 4:00 p.m.

"Wow! What a relief," Burl said to Buddy Bud.

"You got that right, brother," she said. "Let's head home."

They both left the club and hopped into Buddy Bud's Dodge Dart.

On the way home, Buddy Bud inquired, "Where's Audrey?"

"I thought you knew; she's working as a waitress at Congressional Country Club."

"No, I didn't know that. Is she coming over today?"

"I surely hope so, you know that I love her very much."

"I know you do, Burl. I think she's a really great person."

"Cool," Burl replied.

"How do you like working at the club?" Buddy Bud asked.

"I think that it's great, I get to work with some really good people like you, Big Chief, and all the rest of the crew."

"Glad to hear it, brother."

"What're you into for the rest of the day?" she asked.

"Well, I was hoping to see Audrey. He replied.

"Where're you going to?"

"Probably her crib."

"Where does she live and what school does she go to?"

"She lives off of Cranford Drive in Potomac right across from the Falls Road golf course, and she went to Churchill High School."

"Oh really, I didn't know that."

"You know now sis."

"Does she like to play any sports?' Buddy Bud asked.

"Actually, she does, she's a really good lacrosse player."

"Cool."

"Does she have any brothers or sisters?"

"Yup, she has a sister named Gwen and a brother named Ian."

"Yeah, Gwen works as a waitress at the Fish House in Greenbelt."

"How about Ian?"

"He works a Cisco Systems down in Chapel Hill, North Carolina."

"Wow! He must be smart as shit."

"Not really, he smoked too much weed with Fred Glassman."

"Well, that doesn't mean he's stupid, we smoke pot and we're not stupid."

"Yeah, I know. Ian's a cool guy, I love him like a brother."

"Has he ever done acid peyote buttons or cocaine?" she asked.

"Naw, he ain't not that stupid."

"Well, that's good."

"Hey, instead of going over to Audrey's crib, you wanna go swimming at the Peels?"

"Naw, I really wanna see Audrey, I haven't seen her in quite a few days."

"How 'bout tomorrow?"

"Let me ask Audrey and see what she thinks."

"Okay, that's cool."

They returned home from the club around 10:00 p.m. and entered the house.

"Hey, Mom, hey, Pops, Buddy Bud, Big Chief, and myself are home."

"Great. How'd work go today?"

"Pretty rough," responded Burl.

"How so?" replied Big John.

"Man, it was busy as hell, Pops. Buddy Bud had to work a party of eight, and Chief was doing dishes all day."

"Wow! Must have been working your butts off."

"Got those right, Pops. We're tired as hell," responded Burl.

"Well, it's time to relax." Big John said.

"What're you up to tomorrow?" Charlotte asked.

"I'm gonna see Audrey at her house."

"How 'bout you, Buddy Bud and Chief?"

Chief responded, "I'm gonna read the comics and build a couple of model airplanes."

"How 'bout you, Buddy Bud?"

"Think I'm gonna do the *New York Times* crossword puzzle and just relax after a really hard day at work."

"Sounds good," replied Charlotte.

By midnight they all retired to bed. Burl woke up at 8:00 a.m., anxious to see Audrey.

"Morning, Mom. How's it going?"

"Great, Burl. How 'bout you?"

"Great, now that I'm going to see Audrey."

"Wow! You really love Audrey, don't you?"

"Got that right, Mom. I love her to death."

"I know you do son, Audrey's a really special gal."

"Can't wait to see her mom."

"What are you gonna do with her today?"

"I'm thinking we'd go shopping at the mall, she has to pick up her uniform for lacrosse."

"She a good lacrosse player?"

"Are you kidding me, Mom? They won the state championship last year."

"Wow! I didn't know that."

"Well, now you do, Mom."

"Let's move on to more important things. What would you like for breakfast?"

"How about French toast?"

"Sure thing."

"Do we have any confectioner sugar? You know how much I like that on French toast."

"Sure do, son."

"What would you like to drink?"

"How about a nice cold glass of milk, I think that goes really well with sweet stuff."

"Anything else?"

"Glass of Orange juice would be great, gotta get in my vitamin C, also think that I'll have a cup of coffee once I finish my breakfast."

"That's fine dear, I'll get right on it. In the meantime, could you please take Sheba for a walk? She hasn't been walked since last night."

At that, Burl left the kitchen to fetch Sheba in her doghouse.

"Come on, girl, let's go for a walk," he said once he got to the doghouse and leashed her up.

The walk took all about forty-five minutes. Breakfast was ready once Burl returned home.

"Breakfast is ready, Burl."

"Thanks, Mom." He wolfed down his breakfast.

"Shoot, Mom, I was gonna visit Audrey at her house, but I forgot I've got school today."

"Well, you'll just have to do it at a later date."

"I know, Mom, but I was really looking forward to seeing her."

"I'm sure she'll understand that school's much more important the visiting her."

"I guess so."

"What car are you driving to school?"

"I was hoping the Corvair. I think the clutch is going bad on it."

"Well, you better ask your father."

"I will, Mom."

Big John was already in the basement working on the bookshelves that he was building.

"Morning, Pops."

"Morning Burl, what's up?"

"I'm heading out to school and was wondering if I could drive the Corvair?"

"Unfortunately, I don't think you can son, you told me the other day that the brakes are going bad, you'll have to drive the Blue Cloud."

"Well, I guess I have no other choice."

"Don't worry son, I'll have the brakes fixed by the time you get home, and you can drive it over to Audrey's house if you plan on seeing her today."

"Actually, I do plan on seeing her later."

"Then there you go Burl, problem solved."

"Great, Pops, then I'll see you after school."

"Okay, son, have a good day."

"Will do, Pops. Luv ya."

"Likewise, Burl."

At that, Burl shot out of the basement and headed out to the Blue Cloud.

At the end of the driveway, he said to himself, "Shit, I almost forgot my books," and headed back inside the house.

His mom was still in the kitchen cleaning up.

"Mom, I almost forgot my books, you know where they are?"

"Yes, they're in the back bedroom on the desk," she replied.

"Great."

Burl thought to himself, now let me see, what classes do I have today? I think human anatomy and physiology and Introduction to Chemistry.

He then grabbed the appropriate books and headed back out to his car.

On the road, he thought about his upcoming classes, *Oh no, I think chemistry will be really tough, but I think I can handle human anatomy and physiology.*

About a half hour later, he pulled into the MC parking lot and found that the space was open in lot 3, space 69.

Burl then headed out to the sciences building where chemistry was being taught.

Upon entering the building, he found the directory of classes being taught and found out that Chemistry 100 was in room 69. He then proceeded into the classroom.

A man of slight build was in the front of the room. The classroom was packed full of students.

"Good morning, ladies and gentlemen, my name's Bob Coley. And I'll be your instructor for this semester. We'll be covering a lot of chemical concepts, so I hope you enjoy the class. Any questions? Great, then let's get started."

A nerdy dude raised his hand. "Dr. Coley, exactly what will we be covering?"

"Well, you'll learn how to balance chemical equations, atomic mass and numbers, learn Avogadro's number, all about radioisotopes, basic stoichiometry, and all about the noble gasses if time allows."

"Thank you, Dr. Coley.

"No problem. Anyone else have any questions?"

No one raised their hand this time.

"Does anyone know what makes up salt?"

Burl raised his hand. "Isn't it NaCl?"

"That's right." How about other salts?" Coley asked.

"I think CaCl also makes up salt along with LiO_2.

"Right again." Does anyone know what the charge of lithium is?"

"I think it has a charge of +2, which is why you need O_2."

"That's right. Where did you learn all of this?" Coley asked Burl.

"In high school chemistry," replied Burl.

"By the way, what's your name?"

"Burl."

"Very good Burl, for that I'll give you extra credit on the first quiz worth five points."

"Thank you, Dr. Coley."

"No problem."

"Now, does anyone know what a noble gas is?"

Burl raised his hand once again.

"A noble gas is a gaseous element such as helium, neon, argon, krypton, and radon occupying group 0 on the periodic table of chemical elements."

"Wow! I'm thoroughly impressed. For that I'll give you five extra points on our next quiz."

The class lasted a full hour, and it was off to human anatomy and physiology.

Burl then looked at his schedule. His next class was in room 369 on the third floor. He then entered the classroom and immediately noticed a skeleton in the corner of the room. The instructor then entered the room.

"Good morning, class. My name's Dr. Richard Seriani, and I'll be your instructor for this semester. Anyone ever take human anatomy and physiology?"

No one raised their hand.

"Well, you're in for a real treat. The reason I say that is because bones, ligaments, and muscles are essential components that make up the human body. Now, let's get started. Does anyone know what bones make up the body?"

A female student raised her hand. "I know a few."

"What's your name, miss?"

"My name's Alice. Alice Johnson."

"Whatcha got Alice?"

"The radius and ulna are the bones that make up one's forearm. They share the functions that let your arm and wrist move. The ulna is slightly longer than the radius. It's on the medial or pinky side of your forearm."

"Right you are, Alice. Are you familiar with any other bones?"

"Yes, in fact, I do. The lower leg is comprised of two bones, the tibia, and the smaller fibula. The thigh bone or femur is the large upper leg bone that connects the lower leg bones or knee joint to the pelvic bone."

"Right again, Alice," Seriani replied. "You're a very smart gal. How do you know all of this?"

"My father's an orthopedic surgeon," she replied.

"Well, he must be very proud of you. Can anyone describe for me some of the major organs of the body?"

One dude raised his hand.

"Great. What's your name, sir?"

"Name's Bill. Bill Alexander."

"Okay, Bill, go right ahead."

"I know a little bit about the kidney."

"Whatcha got Bill?"

"Internally, the kidney has three regions. An outer cortex, a medulla in the middle, and the renal pelvis in the region called the hilum of the kidney. The hilum is the concave part of the bean shape where blood vessels and nerves enter and exit the kidney. It is also the point of exit for the ureters."

"Very good, Bill. Anyone else?"

A guy with Coke-bottle glasses raised his hand.

"What's your name?"

"Name's Bob. Bob Walton."

"Go ahead, Bob."

"I know a bit about the liver," he responded.

"Okay, go ahead."

"The liver consists of two main lobes; both are made up of eight segments that consist of one thousand lobules or small lobes. These lobules are connected to small ducts to form the common hepatic duct."

"Right you are, Bob."

"Now, does anyone know anything about the brain?"

A nerdy dude wearing a paisley shirt, plaid shorts, and flip-flops raised his hand.

"Okay, sir, what's your name?"

"Earl. Earl Hitchcock."

"Whatcha got, Earl?"

"The brain can be divided into three basic units: the forebrain, the midbrain, and the hindbrain. The hindbrain includes the upper part of the spinal cord, the brain stem, and a wrinkled ball of tissue called the cerebellum. The hindbrain controls the body's vital functions such as respiration and heart rate."

The class lasted forty-five minutes.

"Okay, good work, you guys. Class dismissed."

Finally, Burl thought, time to get the hell out of here and go see Audrey.

Burl then headed to space sixty-nine to get to the Blue Cloud and calls Audrey on his mobile phone.

"Sweetheart, I'm all done with school. Can I come over now?"

"Sure thing, dear. I was waiting for your call."

"Great. I should be at your place in about a half hour."

"Good. See you then."

Burl, excited to see Audrey, floored the gas pedal.

As promised, he turned onto Cranford Drive a half hour later and parked the Blue Cloud in Audrey's driveway and hurriedly rushed to the door to Audrey's home.

Audrey answered the door. "Oh, sweetheart you finally made it."

"Oh my god, what a hell of a day this was."

"What happened, my love?"

"Well, I went to chemistry, and it was tough as shit then I went to human anatomy and physiology, and it was equally as bad."

"Well, why don't you come in and take your shoes off."

"Man, I really need to relax after this horrendous day."

Well, just take it easy and I'll fix you some lunch."

"What do you have sweetheart?"

"How about a Reuben on rye?"

"Sounds great. You want me to help you with it?"

"No, that's okay, I'll fix it myself."

"Great."

Audrey then proceeded into the kitchen to fix Burl his sandwich.

About a half hour later, Audrey entered the living room with Burl's sandwich.

"Here you go dear, enjoy."

"Thanks, sweetheart."

"No problem my love."

Burl proceeded to wolf down his sandwich.

"Thanks, sweetheart. That was great."

"Glad you liked it," she replied.

"Whaddya want to do now sweetheart?"

"I was thinking we could go for a swim at the Peels."

"Cool. Let me call Scottie and see if it's alright."

"Well, he should let you go swimming in his pool given the number of times you've let him go swimming in your pool."

"I know, I know but I still have to check it out with him nonetheless."

Burl then dialed Scottie's number: (301) 424-7769. Scottie answered the phone.

"Hey, Scottie, you think Audrey and I can go for a swim in your pool?"

"Sure thing, buddy. When you think you can come over?"

"Right now, if that's okay."

"No problem, man, see you later."

"Hey, Audrey, Scottie says that it's okay to go for a swim in his pool."

"Good. Let's hit the road."

"Get your swimsuit on sweetheart."

"Okay, my love, also I think that I have your swimsuit from the last time we went swimming at your house."

"Cool."

Then, they both change into their swimsuits.

"Okay, let's go," said Burl.

At that point, they both headed out to the Blue Cloud.

It was a beautiful September day, not a cloud in the sky and the sun was shining brightly.

The two arrived at the Peel's residence a half hour later. Scottie was there waiting for them.

"Hey, Scottie, what's happening?" said Burl.

"Just waiting for you guys to arrive."

"How's the pool water, is it very cold?" asked Burl.

"Naw, it's actually pretty warm given that the temperature has been quite hot lately."

"Can we jump in now?" Audrey asked.

"Yup, it's ready and waiting."

"Then let's do it," replied Burl.

Damn, Burl thought. *Audrey looks so hot in her swimsuit.*

At that, they both jumped into the swimming pool.

"Wow! This feels so good," said Audrey

"You got that right," replied Burl.

"What're you guys doing tonight?" asked Scottie.

"Just having dinner with my folks," replied Burl. "Wanna join us for dinner?" Burl asked.

"Sure, what are you having for dinner?"

"Not quite sure," replied Burl. "Let me call my pops and ask him."

The three of them headed inside Scottie's house. Vicki and Kathy were standing in the kitchen.

"What's happening ladies?" Burl asked.

"Not much," replied Vicki. "What are you guys up to?" Kathy asked.

"Just want to call my pops to see if Scottie can join us for dinner.

Billy then entered the kitchen.

"Hey, guys, how's it going?" he asked.

"Pretty good," replied Burl.

"Come upstairs, I gotta show you guys something."

Burl, Audrey, and Scottie headed upstairs with Billy.

"Check this out."

Billy drops his drawers and lights a match and lets out a huge fart and the gas lights up like a torch.

"Fuck, Billy, I can't believe you'd do this in front of us, especially in front of a lady like Audrey."

"But man, don't you think this is so cool?"

"Not really, you're a damn pervert," said Scottie.

"Sorry Audrey, I just thought that you'd think this pretty cool."

Audrey just looked on in disbelief.

"Okay, enough of this shit. Let's call your pops," replied Scottie.

Scottie, Audrey, and Burl headed back downstairs into the kitchen.

Burl picked up the phone and dialed his parent's number: (301) 424-7769.

Big John answered the phone.

"Hey, Pops, how's it going?"

"Pretty good. How 'bout you, Burl?"

"We're just up at Scotties for a swim. Pops, I was wondering if Scottie could join us for dinner?"

"Sure son, would love to have him over for dinner."

"What are we having?"

"Sirloin on the grill."

"Great. We'll head out now, should be home in about fifteen minutes."

"Great. See you then, Burl."

The three of them proceeded to head outside, and Scottie fired up his minibike that he found in the ditch leading up to his house. The minibike had been abandoned by someone that neither of them knew whose it was.

When they got to the house, they were confronted with the smell of freshly cut grass.

The three of them then entered the porch just inside the garage where Big John and Charlotte were sitting along with Sheba.

"Hey, Mom, hey, Pops, how's it going?"

"Just enjoying the beautiful weather."

"I know, it's awesome, isn't it?" responded Burl.

"Sure, is son, replied Big John. "How was your swim?"

"Great," replied Audrey. "The water was a perfect temperature."

"Ready for dinner?" asked Charlotte.

"Ready and waiting," replied Burl.

"I see that you've been cutting the grass, Pops."

"How's the John Deere running?"

"She purrs like a kitten," Big John replied.

"How's the push mower running?"

"About the same as the John Deere."

"Pops, I can't believe you make us cut the one acre of our property with a push mower."

"Well, it keeps you in shape, doesn't it?"

"I can think of better ways to stay in shape, Pops."

"If that's the case, I'll have to teach you how to cut the grass with the John Deere."

"Thanks, Pops, really appreciate it."

"Hey, son, think you could fire up the grill?"

"Sure thing, Pops."

At that point, Burl headed out back to fire up the Weber grill.

"Hey, Scottie, you wanna help me fire up the grill?"

"Sure thing, Burl," he replied.

"Great. Could you please grab the charcoal out of the garage?"

"Sure thing, my friend."

"Also, can you grab the lighter fluid while you're at it?"

"Yup."

Burl then headed out to the backyard to light up the grill with Sheba in tow.

"How you doing, girl?"

Sheba wagged her tail and answered with a loud bark.

Scottie then returned with the charcoal and lighter fluid. "Here you go, Burl."

"Thanks, man."

Burl then laid down a couple of sheets of newspaper and twigs that he gathered from the maple tree and formed a pyramid with the charcoal.

"You gotta a lighter or a match?" Burl asked.

"Here, I got some matches."

"Cool."

The reason why Scottie had matches was because he smoked cigarettes.

"Dude, fire up the charcoal."

"Don't be so impatient," Burl exclaimed.

"I know. I'm really sorry, man."

Burl then struck up a match and proceeded to light up the charcoal.

"That should do it, buddy. Let's head back into the porch." And with that they did.

Audrey then asked, "Mom, can I help you with dinner?"

"Sure, dear. Let's head into the kitchen."

"Audrey, could you please pull out the sirloin from the fridge?"

"No problem, Mom." As she proceeded to do so.

"Here you go Mom, here's the sirloin. Need anything else?"

"Yes, I wanna brew some tea for ice tea. You can grab the tea-bags from the cupboard above the toaster. The pot to boil the water in is in the cupboard below the sink.

"Gotcha covered Mom."

"Audrey, could you please ask Burl to come in here?"

"Sure thing." Audrey then headed out to the porch to get Burl.

"Hey, Burl, Mom would like to see you in the kitchen."

"Okay, sweetheart, I'll be in right away."

"Hey, Mom, whatcha need?"

"Could you please set the table?"

"Sure thing, Mom. Also, could you ask Scottie if he could walk Sheba? She hasn't been walked in a while."

Burl went back onto the porch.

"Hey, Scottie, my mom was wondering if you could walk Sheba, her leash is hanging up in the garage."

"Sure thing, Burl." Scottie then headed out to the garage to fetch the leash, and then he went out to the doghouse.

"Come on, Sheba, I'm gonna take you for a walk."

Sheba complied without hesitation.

Back in the kitchen, Burl set out to set the table. "Okay, Mom, I'm back."

"Dear, why don't you use the Wedgwood plates? There in the cupboard above the stove."

"Gotcha covered, Mom." Burl then grabbed the plates.

"Burl, could you please ask your father to come in here?"

"Yup." He headed back to the porch. "Hey, Pops, Mom wants to see you in the kitchen."

"Sure thing, son. Whatcha need dear?"

"Could you please throw the sirloin on the grill?"

"Sure thing, sweetheart."

Big John then grabbed the sirloin off the counter where Audrey had left it, and he then headed out to the Weber to throw the steak onto the grill.

In the meantime, Scottie returned from his walk. "Can I help you with anything, Pops?"

"No thanks, I got it all covered."

"Cool. I'll head back inside and see if Burl's mom needs any help."

Scottie then entered the kitchen.

"Hey, Mom, how can I help out?"

"If you could please throw the teabags into the boiling water, that' be a great help."

"Sure thing," he replied.

Now by the grill, Pops threw the sirloin onto the grill.

Back in the kitchen, Audrey asked, "Mom, can I help you with anything else?"

"Yes. Could you please throw five potatoes into the microwave oven?"

"Sure."

"Burl, some people may want sour cream on their potatoes. Could you please grab that along with some butter out of the fridge? Could you please grab some salt and pepper?"

"Sure thing, Mom." Burl did so as instructed. "Mom, I gonna go outside and see how the steak is coming along. Hey, Pops how's it going?"

"Steak's almost done. Let's give another five minutes."

Burl headed back to the kitchen. "Mom, steak's gonna be ready in five minutes."

"Great. Can you please tell Audrey to come in here?"

"Sure thing."

Audrey then entered the kitchen. "Hey, Mom, whatcha need?"

"Could you please get the glasses and set them on the table and fill them up with ice?"

"You got it."

Pops then entered the kitchen. "Steak's done."

"Great, let's gather around the table."

"Let's wait for Scottie. He's still walking Sheba," said Big John.

Scottie then entered the garage, came through the porch, and then entered the dining room.

"How'd the walk go?" asked Burl.

"Just fine, although she did want to go swimming in the Willis Pond, but I didn't let her."

"Ready to eat?" Charlotte asked.

"You bet, that walk made me really hungry."

"Great, then let's dig in," replied Burl.

At that, all five of them take a seat at the table.

"Who wants to say grace?" Charlotte asked.

"I guess I will," said Pops, and he proceeded to do so. "Bless us, Father God, for these thy gifts we're about to receive. And thank you for your kind and generous heart. Amen."

"Nice grace, Pops," said Burl.

"Dear, why don't you cut up the steak," Charlotte said.

"Gladly, sweetheart."

"Can you please pass the potatoes around the table, Audrey, along with the sour cream, salt, and pepper."

"Sure thing, Mom."

They finished eating around 6:45 p.m.

What's on the agenda now?" asked Burl.

"I think *60 Minutes* is on at 7:00 p.m.," said Big John. "You all wanna watch it?"

"Sure," replied Burl.

"What channel's it on?" asked Burl.

“I think it’s on CBS, channel 9,” replied Big John.

“Okay,” replied Burl. I’ll turn it on right now.”

What’s the show about and who’s hosting it?” asked Audrey.

“I think that it’s Dan Rather. Let’s see,” replied Burl. “I’ll turn it on right away.”

Burl proceeded to do so.

“Good evening, ladies and gentlemen,” said Dan Rather. “We have a very good show in store for our viewing audience tonight. “It’s about canine behavior.”

“Cool,” replied Burl.

“We’re going to explore how intellectual dogs are. In particular, Siberian huskies,” Dan responded.

“Wow!” I can’t wait to see this one,” commented Audrey.

By that time Scottie had gone home for the evening.

“Huskies have sensors in hair follicles that are located inside their ears,” said Rather. “And we’re going to explore how they’re able to navigate while using these hair follicles,” he replied.

“This is really cool,” replied Audrey.

Next, they talked about an Alaskan sled dog named Kodei who was a cute little fella with one blue eye and the other brown in color.

The owner named Andrew was leading the discussion.

“What can you tell us about Kodei?” asked Rather.

“Well, at one point Kodei was lost and was found about three miles away. And somehow, he found his way back home.”

A veterinarian named Tim Sorrells was then interviewed.

“Now, Dr. Sorrells, what can you tell us about Kodei’s behavior?” asked Dan.

“Well, Kodei’s a very smart dog.”

“How so?”

“Well, when you ask him to sit or lay down, he readily complies.

“Please go on, Dr. Sorrells.”

“Please let me demonstrate,” said the doctor.

He then commanded Kodei to come, “Come on, boy.”

Kodei responded immediately to the command. Next, Kodei responded by licking Dr. Sorrells’s ears, neck, and face.

"Good boy, Kodei," the doctor said as Kodei demonstrated his prowess.

"Wow! That's quite incredible," commented Rather.

During the fall of 1978, Burl left Lakewood Country Club to wait tables at Pudge's restaurant in Montgomery Village in Gaithersburg, Maryland.

The restaurant was named after Pudge Ruppert. The owner Pudge was a real roly-poly mother fucker. He had a pendulous stomach that hung over his beltline, crow's feet, and a neck that looked like that of a turtle.

Also employed at the restaurant was Mike Blade whom Burl knew from the Family Fish House. Blade worked as a bartender just as he had at the Fish House.

Then there was Lenny who reminded Burl of a monkey. He wore an ill-fitting toupee and had bags under his eyes, a real piece of work.

Working at the restaurant was Craig Rice who Buddy Bud had the hots for at one point in time. Can't forget Bill Johnson who worked as a line cook along with Bruce Milne. Burl knew Milne's sister Lisa while attending St. Mary's College in later years.

On one memorable occasion, Craig and Bill, unbeknownst to Burl, cooked up a batch of weed brownies. At the time, Burl was hungry and consumed a boatload of brownies, not to mention that he became high as shit.

As it turned out, a huge thunderstorm hit Montgomery Village that night and caused a power outage; and Burl of course had to wait table on Pudge, Lenny, and Kathy, Pudge's main squeeze.

Burl couldn't remember anything worth shit and became flustered as hell when trying to fill their order, truly a night to remember.

Working at Pudges was not a loss for Burl however in that it did pay for Burl's education at St. Mary's College.

Burl had some fond memories while attending SMC. He met Special Ed, Chris Baumgardner, Red Cloud, Tim Feinstein, Pete Mosher, and Keith Brace.

One not-so-fond memory was when Burl's roommate Mark Black got racked. To this day, Burl felt guilty about allowing Mark to get racked, after all, Black wasn't that bad of a dude as it turned out.

Every year, the college would host a Frisbee golf tournament. Brace threw a 165-gram Frisbee and would invariably win the tournament. While the tournament was going on, Andy Chavannes would cruise around the campus on a golf cart and serve beer, which was supplied by Peck's a local liquor store. The boys would get fucked up as shit.

Burl couldn't forget the time when he and the boys picked up Mosher's VW Beetle and hauled it behind the Caroline dormitory. Funny.

Then there was the time the Baltimore Orioles were playing the Pittsburg Pirates. The Orioles ended up losing the game which infuriated Burl and Special Ed. As a result, Burl and Special Ed went down to the girl's dormitory (Queen Ann's) and pulled the fire alarm.

No one could mistake Special Ed's bulky physique, and as a result, the two got busted for pulling the alarm. Renwick Jackson, the school's president, insisted that Burl and Special Ed present a fire safety presentation in front of the Dorchester's roommates. They had no choice but were forced to do so. The fire chief from Lexington Park, the closest city to St. Mary's, came in with a slide presentation on fire safety. Burl and Special were so embarrassed over the situation.

Can't forget the time when Jaybird, another one of Burl's roommates, took Burl's VW Beetle onto the soccer.

Becks had supplied the school with about ten kegs of Beer. Burl and Jaybird took Burl's VW and did slaloms around the soccer field doing doughnuts while tearing the field to smithereens.

Burl really enjoyed his time at SMC except for where he lived.

He first lived in the Dorchester dorm, which he really didn't mind, for that's where he met all his good friends. What he did mind was the house he lived in at Ridge.

The house was infested with field mice, it was heated by an antiquated kerosene stove, and the water pipes were installed above the ceiling, something a contractor would never hear of.

On one Thanksgiving holiday, the pipes froze over and filled the bathtub up with ice, enough to go skating on.

He did like the idea that the Hideaway Bar was a stone's throw away from the house. On school nights, beer was offered 25¢ for a sixteen-ounce cup, enough to get blasted on.

It was here that he banged Kathy McPherson and Margo (a.k.a. Cargo).

Cargo and McPherson had big tits, which Burl couldn't get enough of. He banged the living shit out of both.

At the time, Burl was living with Tony Cornish and Tony Hauserman, both of whom he liked. What he didn't like was Dan Haynos's girlfriend named Sue Moss who had severe asthma. In the morning she'd eat a clove of garlic, thinking it would clear up her condition. Burl would have to roll down his window just to get rid of the nasty smell. Unbelievable.

Burl, however, did like his instructors at the college.

First, there was Charlie Krebs, his teacher for estuarine dynamics, followed by Chris Tanner, his nonvascular and vascular botany instructor.

Then there was Bob Eichenmuler, his entomology instructor; followed by Richard Seriani, his microbiology and human anatomy and physiology instructor; and finally Rick Sheridan, his molecular biology instructor.

Burl excelled in all his studies. He got an A+ in all but one of his courses, which was microbiology.

Following SMC, Burl applied to graduate school at UMBC (University of Maryland, Baltimore County), the University of South Carolina (Columbia, South Carolina), and finally the Johns Hopkins University in Baltimore, Maryland.

Fortunately, he got accepted to UMBC even with his meager 3.3 GPA.

Burl was very excited about getting into graduate school. He was first under the tutelage of Dr. Richard Wolf in genetics. In the lab were Mark Nasoff, Barry Jordan, and Henry Baker, whom Burl hated with a passion. The bastard gave Burl shit because he couldn't do a simple serial dilution.

Across the hall from Wolf's lab was Bill Kelly under Phillip Roth and Dave Donovan who later Burl found out was gay as a gay blade, but he still liked Dave, nonetheless.

Upon entering UMBC, Wolf asked Burl if he wouldn't mind teaching freshman genetics.

Burl had no problems with that, so he began teaching that with no questions asked.

On his first day, he was approached by Lisa Molina who asked him for help with her genetics homework. Burl had no problems with that, so he readily complied.

"Okay, what can I help you with dear?"

"I can't get a hang with genetics homework," she said.

"Let me see if I can't help you out, sweetheart."

At that, Burl asked her to open her homework.

"I see what the problem is. You tried dividing the subset of the problem by 9 when it should have been divided by 8."

"Oh really," she replied.

"No problem. Just try not to make the mistake next time."

CHAPTER 8

"Thanks, Burl. I'll be sure to be more careful next time," she replied.

"Quite alright dear."

At that, Lisa was on her way to her next class in humanities.

"Alright class, today we're going to be studying bipolar illness. Anyone have any idea what I'm talking about?"

Some bitch named Susan raised her hand.

"Yes, ma'am, I know exactly what that is."

"Okay, what is it?"

"Well, it's when an individual can't control their impulse to gamble."

"Right you are, anything else?"

"Yes, in fact, there is something else.

"Okay, let's have it."

"Well, just as you can see, because they show the symptoms of obsessive-compulsive behavior doesn't mean that they're afflicted with the disorder."

"Right you are, anything else?"

"No, not really."

"Great. Anyone else have something to add to the discussion?"

No one else raised their hand.

"Okay, class dismissed."

At that, the class left the room, moving on to their next class, which was biology.

"Okay, ladies and gentlemen, you know what time it is?" It's time you learn something about Mendelian genetics."

Fuck, Burl thought to himself, *this class is gonna be hard as shit.*

And so it was. Burl just couldn't get a hang of the stuff being taught no matter how hard he tried.

"Oh well, guess I'll get through it somehow," he said to himself, and so he did.

The class lasted a full three hours before it was over.

Damn, I'm glad the class is over, he thought. He then cruised over to his next class in the humanities building. *Man, I'm tired as shit. Can't wait until the next class is over.*

It was 3:30 p.m. when Burl finally got out of class.

Man, I miss Audrey so much. I must go see her. He then climbed into the Blue Cloud and was off to see the love of his life.

He arrived at Audrey's crib at around 4:00 p.m.

"Sweetheart, I'm here."

"Oh dear, I missed you so very much."

"I missed you as well Sweetheart."

Whaddya want to do my love?"

"I was thinking we could go over to my folks for dinner."

"That'd be okay, but my mom's already cooked us dinner."

"Well, I guess that's okay, but I'll have to phone my parents and let them know that we won't be showing up."

"That's cool," Audrey replied.

Burl then dialed the number 424-399-7769. Pops answered the phone.

"Hey, Pops, how's it going?"

"Just fine, son. Where are you?"

"I'm over at Audrey's house and I'm gonna have dinner here."

"Aww, that's too bad, Burl. Mom's fixing your favorite dinner, pepper steak."

"Well, I guess that we'll just have to make it another time."

"Man, Pops, I'm really sorry."

"That's okay, son. Like you said, we'll just have to do it at some other time."

"Okay, Pops, I'll catch you later."

"What time do you think you'll be home, Burl?"

"Not too late, probably around 9:00 p.m. I've got school tomorrow."

"Great. See you then, son."

"Okay, Audrey, I just talked to Pops, and he said that it's okay if I stay for dinner."

"Great. I'll let my mom know."

"Know what she's having for dinner?"

"I think beef Wellington.'

"Wow! Never had it before, is it any good?"

"Damn right, my mom makes the best."

"Cool. Can't wait to try it."

"By the way, where's Ian?"

"I think that he's visiting Fred Glassman, but I'll check with my mom."

"Alright, sweetheart, you just do that."

Audrey then left the room and returned shortly to Burl in the living room area where Burl was sitting.

"Yeah, I was right, Ian's visiting Fred."

"Meant to ask you, sweetheart, you got any weed?"

"Sure do, I just copped some from Betsy, you wanna smoke some?"

"Do I ever, I haven't gotten stoned in a long time."

"Great. Let's go into the garage." And the two of them proceeded to do so.

"Sweetheart, you got any papers or a pipe?"

"Shit, I almost forgot. Let me check Ian's room. He and Fred get stoned all the time."

Audrey left the garage for several minutes.

"We're In luck dear, Ian had a chamber pipe in his dresser drawer."

"Cool, then let's spark up a bowl."

Burl pulled a Bic lighter out of his pocket.

"Here you go sweetheart, spark that bitch up."

Audrey proceeded to do so.

"Here you go, dear. Take a hit."

"Gladly," replied Burl.

Burl took a huge draw on the pipe, inhaled, and then exhaled the smoke.

"Man Audrey, this is some really good shit, where'd Betsy get it from?"

"Her brother Bobby."

"We gotta get some more of this weed, sweetheart. How much was it?"

"It's $69."

"Wow! That's a really good price, was it an ounce?"

"No, it was a three-fingered lid."

"That's still a very good price, when can we cop some?"

"Just about any time, just give me the word and I'll score some."

"How 'bout tomorrow?"

"Sure, I'll buy it for you as an early birthday present."

"You don't have to sweetheart; I can buy my own."

"I know you have the money, but just consider it a special treat."

"Okay, if you say so, sweetheart."

"Can't wait to taste that beef Wellington that your mom's making."

"Let me go check and see when dinner will be ready."

"Sweetheart, wait, your eyes are really red. You don't want your mom to know that you're getting stoned."

"Good point. Got any VISINE?"

"Yup, right here in my pocket."

"Cool. Can you please put it in my eyes for me?"

"Sure thing, my love." Burl then squeezed a few drops in each of Audrey's eyes. "Good to go, sweetheart."

"Thanks, Burl." Audrey then left the garage. Several minutes later she returned to Burl. "Dear, Mom says dinner will be ready in about ten minutes. Are my eyes still red?"

"No, they're all cleared up."

"Cool."

"By the way sweetheart, where's Ian?"

"Must still be at Fred's. I'll give him a call right now. He's gotta come home for dinner. Beef Wellington's one of his favorite meals."

At that, Audrey was off to the kitchen to use the phone.

She thought to herself, *Now, what's Fred's phone number? Oh, here it is. It's (301) 774-3469.*

Mrs. Glassman answered the phone.

"Hello, Mrs. Glassman, is Ian there?"

"Sure thing. Let me get him for you."

Ian picked up the phone.

"Hello, Ian, dinner's almost ready. Can you come home now? Mom's fixing beef Wellington, one of your favorites."

"Sure thing, sis. I'm on my way."

Ian arrived at the house about fifteen minutes later and entered the front door.

"Hey, sis, hey Burl what's happening?"

"Not much Ian just waiting for you to get home," replied Audrey. "How's Fred doing?"

"Not bad, but the reefer he had was pretty bad."

"Who'd he get it from?" asked Audrey. "Couldn't have been Bobby. His weed is good."

"I wish you'd have told me earlier or else Fred wouldn't have wasted his money."

"Well, you live, and you learn Ian," replied Burl.

"Yeah, I know, but it doesn't make the situation any easier to handle."

"Don't worry, brother. Just cop some weed from Bobby. It's some really good shit."

"How much does he have to sell?" replied Ian.

"Well, your sister just got some, a three-fingered lid."

CHAPTER 9

Burl decided that they want to go to Gordon Ramsay's restaurant in the National Harbor in Prince George's County, Maryland. So he contacted Jacklaun to see if she'd be interested in going.

Burl then called up Jacklaun: (301) 774-3415.

She then picked up the phone.

"Hey, Jacklaun, you wanna go to Gordon Ramsay's Hell's Kitchen?"

"Sure, when do you wanna go?"

"I was thinking about tomorrow at 7:30 p.m.," said Burl.

"Great, then you gotta date," replied Jacklaun.

The next day rolled around. Burl, Jacklaun, and Bridget decide to go along as well. It was 7:30 p.m.

Burl, Jacklaun, Carl, and Bridget entered the restaurant.

"Mom, maybe we'll get to meet Gordon Ramsay himself," said Carl.

"Highly unlikely," replied Jacklaun. "But you never know we may get lucky."

The restaurant was some classy shit—subzero freezer and refrigerator, a forty-eight-inch Thermador Dual Fuel Professional range, and finally a forty-eight-inch Thermador Dual Fuel stove.

"Good afternoon, ladies and gentlemen," Gordon said in his thick British accent. "As you may already know, my name's Gordon

Ramsay, and I'll be your lead chef for the day. And accompanying me will be my assistant chef Sophia. Now let's get started."

Jacklaun said, "Man, I'm about to shit my pants."

"Me too," replied Burl.

"Now," said Ramsay, "here are the ingredients that we'll be using to prepare my classic beef Wellington."

2 pounds of center-cut beef tenderloin
2 tablespoons of extra virgin olive oil
1 cup of domestic and portabella mushrooms
1/2 cup of Madeira wine
1 puff pastry sheet and flour for dusting
6 slices of prosciutto ham
1 tablespoon of Dijon mustard
1 whisked egg
kosher salt and pepper to taste
kosher salt and fresh cracked to taste
chopped chives for garnish

"Also, the oven must be preheated to four hundred degrees Fahrenheit," Ramsay said.

"Wow! Check it out," said Burl. "Gordon really knows his shit when it comes to kitchen appliances."

"Clearly," replied Jacklaun.

They all take their seats.

A female chef then entered the kitchen.

"Now, ladies and gentlemen, my name's Sophia. I'll be your assistant chef for the day. Gordon will be the lead chef."

"Mom, unbelievable. We're actually gonna see Gordon. Isn't that wonderful?" said Carl.

"Well, I guess you're right, this is our lucky day Carl."

"I can't wait to meet him," replied Carl.

Ramsay then entered the kitchen.

"Wow! This is gonna be some awesome shit," Burl excitedly stated.

"You bet your socks off," replied Jacklaun.

"Now, enough said, let's get started," said Ramsay.

"Sophia, why don't you gather the ingredients while I chat with the audience and pour them a little wine," replied Ramsay.

"Surely," replied Sophia.

"Now, what are your names?" Gordon asked.

"Well, Gordon, my name's Jacklaun. This is my daughter, Carl. This is my niece, Bridget. And this is my brother. His name's Burl.

"Great to meet you, folks. Now, have any of you ever cooked beef Wellington?" Gordon asked the three of them. They all nod to the negative.

"Good, then you're in for a real treat."

"Now, on to the wine. Jacklaun, would you like white or red wine? I'd suggest red. It goes best with the Wellington. Burl, how about you?"

"Red as well, Gordon."

"Carl, how about you?"

"No thanks, Mr. Ramsay. I don't drink alcohol," Carl responded. "But I will take a glass of water."

"Dear, you don't have to call me Mr. Ramsay. Gordon will do just fine."

"Thank you, Gordon."

Ramsay then poured out the drinks and turned to Sophia. "Sophia, how're coming with the ingredients?" Gordon asked.

"Just fine, Gordon. I'm almost done," she replied.

"Then why don't we get right on it."

"Okay, would anyone from our viewing audience like to assist Sophia?" replied Ramsay. "Carl, why don't you help Sophia out."

"Certainly, Gordon."

"How're we looking, Sophia?" asked Ramsay inquired.

"Ready to go, Gordon," she responded.

"Carl, why don't you get us started?"

"Thank you, Gordon!"

"Now, what would you like me to do Gordon?"

"Why don't you let Sophia tell you?"

"Sophia, what can I do to help?"

"Just parse out the ingredients and pour them into this bowl."

"Certainly, Sophia," replied Carl.

Carl parsed out the ingredients.

"Ready to go," stated Sophia.

"Great. We must first marinate the tenderloin for a few minutes."

Carl then placed the tenderloin into the bowl.

"Okay, everyone set on their drinks?"

Everyone nodded in the affirmative.

Sophia now chimes in.

"Carl, why don't you wrap the tenderloin with the Prosciutto ham?"

"Sure, Sophia."

Jacklaun then raised her hand.

"Gordon, are you making any sides with the Wellington?"

"Yes, in fact, Sophia's gonna make garlic mashed potatoes.

"Thank you, Gordon."

"Certainly Jacklaun."

"Carl, how're we doing?" asked Gordon.

"Think that we're about ready, Gordon," she replied.

"Great. Now, throw it in the preheated pan that Sophia has prepared for you."

"Will do Gordon."

"Now, we're gonna cook it for about forty-five minutes and it should be done."

Burl then raised his hand.

"Gordon, how long do we cook the tenderloin for?"

"Well, it's really up to you, but I prefer a medium rare done tenderloin."

"Yeah, that's how I like it, Gordon."

Exactly forty-five minutes and the tenderloin was done cooking.

"Now, who would like to taste the final product? Carl, why don't you?"

"Certainly, Gordon."

Sophia cuts off a thin slice and forks it over to Carl.

"Here you go, Carl. Try it out."

"Wow! This really tastes delicious Sophia."

"I thought that you'd like it, Carl."

"Sure do, Gordon. You hit the nail right on the head."

The show lasted a full hour, and then they were done.

"Now, as a celebratory gesture let's have a glass of French champagne."

And that they did. Time to leave after the toast.

"Thank you all for coming," stated Gordon.

As they left the restaurant, Burl stated, "Man, that was really excellent."

"Right on," replied Jacklaun. And off they were.

Finally home, Jacklaun said, "That was really excellent."

"Tell me about it," responded Burl.

"Guys, I don't know about you, but I'm really beat as hell. I'm going to bed."

"Me too," replied Jacklaun. "Burl, you wanna spend the night at my house?"

"Damn right, Jacklaun."

"Good, then let's get on our way. Where'd you park the Blue Cloud?" she asked.

"Space sixty-nine on the waterfront.

"Cool, then why don't we head out now."

After spending the night at Jacklaun's house, Burl then headed over to Audrey's house, the love of his life.

Audrey was very concerned about Ian's behavior as of late.

Audrey entered Ian's room.

"What's going on, Ian?" He had a poster of Cheryl Tiegs, scantily clad, hanging on his wall.

"Not much just getting stoned," replied Ian.

"Is Sterling Nuts here?" It was a name he lovingly called Burl.

"Yeah, he's in the living room with Mom," replied Audrey.

"Are my eyes red?"

"Yeah, they're red as shit."

"Here, here, here's some VISINE. That should clear up your eyes."

"Cool, sis. You're the best," responded Ian.

"Don't know about that, but get your ass into the living room."

"Will do," her brother replied.

Ian then entered the living room.

What's happening guys?"

"Just waiting for you," replied Burl.

"What's for dinner?" asked Audrey.

"Dijon mustard chicken along with white rice," replied Anne. "What to drink?"

"Ice tea and lemonade," replied Anne.

"Need any help, Mom, fixing dinner?" asked Audrey.

"Sure do."

"If you or Burl please set the table, that'd be a great help."

"Sure thing, Mom," replied Audrey.

Audrey then entered the living room and approached Burl.

"Dear, could you please help me set the table?"

"Sure honey bunch."

Burl and Audrey then entered the kitchen.

"Mom, Burl and I are here to help. You want us to set the table, don't you?"

"Sure Audrey, that'd be a great help," replied Anne

Burl and Audrey then proceeded to set the table in accordance with Anne's request.

"Please use the Wedgewood plates, and please don't forget to set the silver flatware."

The two of them proceeded into the kitchen.

"Mom, where are the plates?"

"Above the oven where they're normally kept," replied Anne.

"How about the flatware?"

In the drawer below the countertop on the left-hand side of the cupboard."

"Great, we'll get right on it," replied Burl.

"Hey, Audrey, why don't you get the plates and I'll get the flatware."

"Sure thing, dear."

At that, the two of them proceeded to carry out the task at hand.

In the meantime, Anne prepared the chicken Dijon.

"How long is the dinner take to prepare?" asked Audrey.

"About forty-five minutes, enough time for you two to have the table set up."

After the table was set, dinner was ready.

"Are you all ready to eat?" Anne asked.

"Sure thing," replied Burl, Audrey and Ian.

"Then come to the table," responded Anne.

"I don't know about you, guys, but I'm hungry as shit," Burl said.

"Me too," replied Audrey.

"Yeah, I'm hungry as hell," replied Ian.

They all proceeded to sit down at the table. No grace was said, for Anne was an atheist; she didn't have a religious thread in her moral fabric.

"What would you all like to drink?" asked Anne.

"I'll take a Diet Coke," replied Audrey, "I gotta watch my weight."

"Aww, come on, Audrey. You have a beautiful figure. You work out just about every day," replied Burl.

"I know, but I still gotta be careful."

"How about you two?" asked Anne.

"I'll take ice tea if you have any," replied Burl.

"Sure do."

"How 'bout you, Ian? What would you like to drink?"

"I'll take Hawaiian punch if we have any."

"Sure do," replied Anne.

They all then proceeded to eat their dinner.

"Wow! This is delicious, Mrs. Burdick," replied Burl.

"How about you two? What do you think?"

"I think that it's great, Mom," replied Ian.

"How about you, Audrey? What do you think?"

"Same," she replied.

"Where'd you get the recipe, Mrs. Burdick?" Burl inquires.

"It's an old family recipe, handed down by Audrey's grandfather Pepe who was French."

"By the way, how are Meme [Audrey and Ian's grandmother who was British] and Pepe doing, Mrs. Burdick?" asked Burl.

"Just fine, thanks for asking. They're living down in Boca Grande in Florida. They're both retired as you may know."

"Yeah, I know that. Audrey told me that."

They all finished dinner about an hour later and decided to watch some TV; it was Sunday night.

"What's on the tube?" Audrey asked.

"Let me check out the TV guide," replied Ian.

A couple of minutes passed by.

"Looks like *60 Minutes*."

"Cool. What's it about?" Inquires Burl.

"Looks like it's a documentary on Alaska," Ian replied.

"Great' let's watch that," replied Audrey. "What channel's it on?"

"Looks like CBS channel 9."

"Who's hosting the show?" asked Burl.

"Dan Rather."

The camera then honed in on Rather.

"That's cool as hell," replied Ian.

The camera then panned out to the Arctic Circle.

"The information that we're about to present to you today was conducted by dozens of researchers throughout the country. They've interviewed world-renowned scientists and a host of specialists in the construction field, engineers, biologists, marine biologists, geologists, meteorologists, ornithologists, and even cartographers.

"As you can see, global warming has severely impacted the polar bears' habitat," said Rather. Their habitat is limited to ice flows from calving glaciers.

"The polar bear is a hyper carnivorous bear whose native range lies largely within the encompassing the Arctic Ocean. Its surrounding seas and surrounding land masses, this includes the most northern regions of North America and Eurasia."

"Wow! Those poor bears," said Audrey. "How're they expected to survive under such harsh conditions?"

"I don't know, sweetheart," replied Burl. "Unless global warming stops, they won't have a snowball chance in hell, no pun intended."

Rather then changed the topic and began talking about the Alaskan pipeline.

"The pipeline project began in April 1974 and finished in June 1977. A total of seventy thousand people were involved in building the line. The pipeline is operated by Alyeska Service, 29 percent. Company [Alyeska], on behalf of its five owners, ConocoPhillips owns.

"Wow! That's unbelievable," replied Burl.

"Sure is," Ian replied.

"Now, let's move on to traveling in Alaska," Rather said. "We'll start our journey in Anchorage, which is about forty-three hours [2,260.1 miles] away from Seattle, Washington. From Anchorage, we then go to Seward, which is two hours and twenty-seven minutes [126.5 miles] away.

"Seward is a short train ride from Anchorage. Along the way, you'll see Dall Sheep [*Ovis dalli dalli*], which inhabit the mountain ranges of Alaska. These white creatures are most notable for the males' massive curled horns. Females [known as ewes] also carry horns, but theirs are shorter than the males.

"Now we'll talk about puffins, which are any of three species of small alcids in the *Fratercula*. These are seabirds that feed primarily by diving in the water. Furthermore, they breed in large colonies on coastal cliffs or offshore islands, nesting in crevices among rocks or burrows in the soil."

Rather then proceeded with his presentation, "Next, we'll present information on walruses. These marine mammals are extremely sociable, prone to loudly bellowing and snorting at one another but are aggressive during mating season. Walruses are distinguished by their long white tusks, grizzly whiskers, flat flipper, and bodies full of blubber.

"Finally, we're going to present information on the whales that inhabit Alaskan waters. Belugas and bowheads inhabit the Artic and subarctic while humpback, fin, blue, minke, and gray whales stick to more southern waters.

"Ladies and gentlemen, that concludes today's edition of *60 Minutes*. Goodbye. Until next week's edition of *60 Minutes*."

"Wow! What a great show that was." Burl exclaims.

"Yeah, it really was," replied Audrey.

"I don't know about you, Audrey, but I'm tired as hell. You wanna go to bed now?"

"Sure thing, dear."

"Mom, Burl and I would like to tuck in now."

"Alright, I've got my bed all made up for you."

"Great," replied Audrey. "What are you gonna do, Mom?"

"I'm going up to the Lewis's to see Bin."

"Damn," Burl said to himself, "I knew she was banging Bin."

"Ian, what are you gonna do?" asked Audrey.

"Think that I'm gonna visit Fred."

"Okay, but don't be too long, you've got school tomorrow."

"I know, I know, sis. Please don't remind me."

"Well, if I don't remind you no one else will."

"That's cool." And off Ian was to visit Fred.

Anne left the house about fifteen minutes later.

"Burl you wanna get stoned?" asked Audrey.

"Never thought you'd ask."

"Good. Let's go into the garage and smoke some weed."

Audrey then left the living room to get the weed from her bedroom.

"You got the reefer?" asked Burl.

"Sure do, dear. Let's go into the garage." And off they were.

In the garage. Burl asked. "You got papers sweetheart?"

"Sure do here."

Burl rolls up a joint.

"Fire that puppy up."

"Sure thing, dear," replied Audrey.

Burl then pulled out his Zippo lighter.

"Here you go sweetheart, take a toke."

"Gladly."

Audrey then took a huge pull on the joint and begins to cough.

"Dear, this is some really strong pot, why am I coughing so much?"

"I know. It's not very good. It's got a lot of stems and seeds in it. I got it from Kevin."

"Well then, I'd suggest you look for a different supplier."

"Got any ideas of who'd be a better supplier?" she asked.

"Yeah, in fact, I do. I think Betsy's brother Bobby might have better weed."

"Oh yeah, when can we cop some?"

"Just about any time, just give me the word."

"How about tomorrow?"

"Unfortunately, that's the only time I can't get it, Bobby's in school."

"Oh really, what school's he in?"

"Drexel University in Pennsylvania."

"He must be smart as shit," replied Burl.

"Not really. He flunked out of Churchill High School."

"Could've fooled me."

"Well, looks can be deceiving," said Audrey.

"Let's go to bed, sweetheart."

"Sure thing."

And off they were to bed. Before they went to sleep, Burl asked Audrey if they should call Fred to see if Ian got there okay. Audrey then picked up the phone to call Fred's house: GA4-7869.

Mrs. Glassman picked up the phone.

"Mrs. Glassman, is Ian over there?"

"Sure is. Would you like to speak with him?"

Ian got on the phone.

"Ian, what are you doing? I told you to get home in a jiff."

"I know, I know, but Fred and I are having a good time."

"That may be true, but good time or not, I told you to be home soon, you've got school tomorrow."

"Okay, okay, I'm heading out now."

"Good, then I expect you home in about ten minutes."

"Whatever you say, sis. You're the boss."

"Good. I'll see you then," replied Audrey.

"Finally, we can get some sleep."

"Good night, Audrey."

"Good night, Burl. Sleep tight."

The two of them fell asleep almost immediately.

At 9:30 a.m., they both woke up. It was a sultry Monday morning.

"How'd sleep, my love?

"Great, Audrey. How 'bout you?"

"Same."

"Wasn't that a good *60 Minutes* last night?"

"Sure was. Dan Rather really knows his shit."

"I gotta get Ian up, he's already late for school."

"He must have smoking weed with Fred.

"Go right ahead, sweetheart."

Audrey knocks on Ian's door.

"Ian, get the hell up, you're late for school."

"Fuck, do I have to?" I'm tired."

"I don't give a flying fuck. If you don't, Mom's gonna put you on restriction."

"Alright, alright, alright already. I'm getting up now."

"Do you want me to fix you some breakfast?"

"Sure, what do we have?"

"Pretty much just cereal."

"What kind do we have?"

"Kix, Cap'n Crunch, Special K, and Rice Krispies."

"I'll go with the Cap'n Crunch."

"Anything else?"

"Sure. How about a glass of orange juice?"

"Anything else, you little shithead?"

"Please don't call me shithead or else Mom will put you on restriction!"

"Okay, just get your ass out of bed."

"Will do, sis."

"By the way, Ian, did you get stoned with Fred last night?"

"Why? What's it matter to you?"

"It matters everything. If you don't quit getting stoned, you'll get kicked out of school."

"No worries. I got a B+ average in all my courses."

"B+ or not, you better get your act straightened out."

"If you think that you're so good, what's your grade point average?"

"Better than yours. I've got an A+ in all my courses."

"Well, aren't you the cat's meow."

"Listen, just eat your breakfast and shut the fuck up."

"Where's Burl?" He'll back me up."

"No, he won't. He thinks that you're a real dipshit.'

"You're the dipshit."

"Whatever, just eat your fucking breakfast."

"How about some toast, or is that too much to ask?"

"Yes, it is. Just eat."

Burl then entered the kitchen.

"What's happening, Ian?"

"Not much. Audrey's just giving me a boatload of shit."

"What about?"

"She thinks that I'm getting stoned too much."

"Well, are you?"

"I don't think so, Fred and I just smoked one joint."

"Yeah, but if you keep it up you're gonna flunk out of school."

"Wow! You sound just like my mother."

"Like it or not, you gotta quit smoking so much weed."

"Easier said than done, Burl."

"Well, I'd suggest you try."

"Alright, alright, but it won't be easy."

"Just try it out and see how you do."

"Cool."

Audrey then entered the conversation.

"Hey, dear, how're doing?"

"Just chatting with Ian."

"Oh yeah, what about?"

"He was just telling me how you're getting so pissed off about him smoking too much reefer."

"Well, it's true. That's all he and Fred do. He needs to do so in moderation."

"I agree."

"If he doesn't chill out, he's gonna flunk out of school."

"You couldn't be more accurate," replied Burl.

The front door to the house opened.

Anne then entered the kitchen with a smile on her face.

"How're you all doing?"

Burl chuckled to himself. She must be smiling because she just fucked Bin.

"Ian, how're doing?" she asked.

"Just fine, Mom. How 'bout you?"

"I had a really great time at the Lewis's.

"That's good. How's Bin doing?"

"Pretty good, but he and Suzanne got into a fight just as I was leaving."

"You know what it was about?"

"Yeah, he and Suzanne were getting into a fight about Bill not wanting to pursue a career in hockey."

"Well, why doesn't he?"

"He wants to drive a Zamboni for a living."

"What's wrong with that, Mom?"

"Because you can get a high school student to do that."

"Yeah, I guess you're right."

"What are you having for breakfast, Ian?"

"Audrey fixed me a bowl of Cap'n Crunch."

"Anything else?"

"A glass of orange juice, she didn't want to serve me toast."

"Why not?"

"I don't know, I guess she's just lazy."

"Audrey, why didn't you want to serve your brother some toast?"

"Because he was being a smart-ass."

"Makes no difference, if he's hungry you have to feed him."

"Well, tell him to quit being such a smart-ass," replied Audrey.

"It's true Ian, your sister takes very good care of you, you really have to ease up a little."

"Okay, Mom, I promise that I will."

"Burl, did you get something to eat?"

"No, but I'll catch a bite at school."

"How 'bout you, Audrey? Did you have anything to eat?"

"No, but just like Burl, I'll catch a bite at school."

"Great. Sounds like you're all set."

Ian finished his breakfast at 10:00 a.m., at which point they hear a bus pull up in front of the house.

"Gotta run guys, the bus just pulled up."

"Okay, Ian, have a good day at school," Anne said.

"Will do, Mom."

Ian then left the house.

"So what do you two have planned for the day?"

"We gotta go to school as well, Mom."

"How're you doing in school Burl?"

"Pretty good, I just got an A+ in my Introduction to Chemistry class."

"Wow! That's great."

"How 'bout you, Audrey? How're you getting along?"

"Pretty good, Mom. I'm working on a B+ in algebra."

"Wow! That's great as well."

"How're you two getting to school today?"

"I think that we're gonna take Burl's Blue Cloud," replied Audrey.

"How's the Blue Cloud running Burl?"

"Great, although I think that it may need new brakes."

"You gonna change them yourself?"

"Naw, my pops gonna change them."

"By the way, how're your mother and father doing?"

"Great. Thanks for asking."

"What's your father doing?"

"Crossword puzzles as usual."

"How 'bout your mom?"

"Just fine, but she has a lot of laundry to do as can be expected given we have a family of ten."

"I'll have to have them mover for dinner sometime. What do they like to eat?"

"Just about anything although my father really loves his sirloin."

"How about your mom? What does she like to eat?"

"She makes a really good bacon and spinach quiche."

"Oh really?"

"Yup."

"Well, you two better get along at school."

"Mom, you know where my books are?"

"Yes, they're in the closet by the front door."

"Thanks, Mom."

"Certainly, dear."

At that point, the two left for school.

The Blue Cloud was parked in Audrey's driveway.

"Hey, sweetheart you wanna drive?"

"No thanks, Burl. Why don't you take the wheel if you said the brakes are going bad? You better drive."

"You're right, sweetheart. I just wasn't thinking straight."

They then cruised down Falls Road to school. About a half hour later, they arrived at school.

"What's your first class, Audrey?"

"Algebra. How 'bout you?"

"Introduction to Chemistry."

"What time you think you're gonna be done?"

"Probably around ten thirty."

"Great. You wanna go to lunch at Hash Brothers?"

"Sure thing, sweetheart," replied Burl.

"Where should we meet?"

"How 'bout outside the humanities building?"

"Yeah, that's fine."

"Great. See you then, sweetheart."

"How about a kiss goodbye?"

"Sure thing, my love."

Burl gave Audrey a light peck on her cheek.

"See you later sweetheart."

"I love you."

"I love you as well, sweetheart."

At that, the two headed off to class. School let out at 12:00 p.m. Burl immediately headed out to the humanities building. Audrey was waiting for him when he got there.

"How was algebra, sweetheart?"

"Pretty tough."

"How so?"

"Well, first we talked about Monomial which has only one nonzero term. Then we talked about binomial, which has two nonzero terms, and finally polynomial, which has more than one nonzero term with nonnegative integral exponents."

"Wow! That seems quite complicated."

"Well, it is. I don't know how I'm ever going to get through it."

"Don't worry, sweetheart, you will. You're smart as shit."

"I certainly hope you're right."

"Ready for lunch?"

"Absolutely."

"Then let's go."

"Where's the Blue Cloud parked?"

"Space sixty-nine in lot three."

"Why are you so enamored with the number 69 anyway?"

"Because it's the love number."

"Speaking of love, you wanna make love to me later?"

"Do I ever."

"Great, then we can do so after lunch."

"Won't your mom be home?"

"Nope, she'll be at work at Sachs Fifth Avenue."

"Cool, then let's be on our way."

They arrived at Hash Brothers around 12:30 p.m.

As they hop out of the Blue Cloud, Burl asked, "Hey, Audrey, what're gonna order for lunch?"

"The usual, pork BBQ. How about you?"

"The usual as well, pot roast and mashed potatoes with a side of Cole slaw."

"Cool."

A waitress approached their table.

"Good afternoon, folks. How are you doing today?"

"Great. How 'bout you?" Burl asked.

"Just fine, thanks for asking."

"Now, can I get you two something to drink?"

"Sure.'

"What would you like?" The waitress asked Burl.

"I'll take a ginger ale."

"And you, ma'am, what can I get you?"

"I'll have a ginger ale as well."

"You know what you'd like to order?"

"Sure."

"Okay, what'll it be?"

"I'll take pot roast with mashed potatoes and a side of Cole slaw."

"And you, ma'am?"

"I'll take the BBQ sandwich."

"Any type of bread?"

"Yes, I'll take it on a kaiser roll if you have it."

"Sure do, anything else?"

"Audrey, are you good with that?" Burl asked.

"Yup, that about does it."

"Great. Your order should be ready in about twenty minutes."

"Thank you, miss."

"No problem."

Wow! I'm tired!" said Burl.

"Me too dear. Can't wait to get home."

"I know you said that your mom wouldn't be home. How 'bout Ian? He can't be home if you want to make love to me."

"Well, we'll have to make sure that he isn't, I'll tell him that he has to go visit Fred."

"Think he'll go for it?"

"Are you kidding? He wants to get stoned all the time."

"Cool."

About twenty minutes later, their waitress arrived with their lunch.

"Here you go, sir, pot roast for you and BBQ sandwich for you, miss."

"Thank you."

"By the way, what's your name?" Burl asked.

"Name's Jennifer. Jennifer Hackman."

"You're not related to Gene Hackman, are you?"

"No. I wish. If I was, I wouldn't be working here."

"Well, just thought that I'd ask."

"Please enjoy your meal," Jennifer said.

"Will do, sweetheart."

At that point, Jennifer left the table.

"Wow! This looks great, doesn't it dear?"

"Sure does, sweetheart. Let's chow down."

The two, hungrier than hell, ate as though they hadn't eaten in about a year.

"Shit, she forgot our drinks," replied Burl. "I'll flag down the busboy."

A busboy then approached their table.

"Excuse me, man, could you please ask Jennifer to come here?"

"Sure thing, sir. I'll get her right away."

At that, the busboy was off to the kitchen to retrieve Jennifer.

Several moments later, Jennifer approached their table.

"Yes sir, what can I get you?"

"I'm sorry Jennifer, but you forgot our drinks."

"Oh damn, I'll get them right away. Two ginger ales, right?"

"That's right Jennifer."

"I'll be back right away."

Jennifer then left the table.

"Wow! This is good dear," replied Audrey.

"Sure is," responded Burl. "Let's chow down." And that they did. They finished their lunch around 2:00 p.m.

"Want anything for dessert?" asked Burl.

"Flag Jennifer down and see what they have."

"Sure thing."

Moments later, Jennifer arrived at their table.

"Sorry about the mishap with the drinks. Can I get you guys anything else?"

"What do you have for dessert?" inquires Burl.

"Well, we have strawberry shortcake, carrot cake, and cherry pie. Can I get you something?"

"I'll take the strawberry shortcake," replied Burl.

"If you don't mind, I'll take the cherry pie," said Audrey.

"Gotcha, anything else?"

"Audrey, you okay with that?"

"Absolutely."

"Great. I'll be back in a jiff."

Jenifer then left the table.

"I know that you said algebra's not going too well with you. How 'bout your other classes Audrey?"

"Pretty good, I really like psychology."

"Oh yeah, what're you studying?"

"Schizophrenia."

Wow! Tell me a little bit about it."

"Well, it's a mental condition involving a breakdown in the relation between thought, emotion, and behavior leading to a full perception of inappropriate actions and feelings, withdrawal from reality and personal relationships into fantasy and delusion and a sense of fragmentation."

"Wow! That's really a mouthful."

"I know, but I definitely like the subject matter," replied Audrey.

"How 'bout your other classes?"

"I really like business and finance along with accounting. I think that I'm gonna major in business."

"Really, that's a change."

"I know, but I like dealing with numbers."

"Cool."

"Anything else?"

"Yeah, I really like PE, given that I like lacrosse and all."

"Wow! You're a busy woman."

"I know, but it keeps me out of trouble."

"Trouble? What trouble?"

"I don't quite know. Maybe having sex and smoking weed."

"Listen, everybody smokes a little weed now and then, even your brother. He's only thirteen years old."

"Yeah, I guess you're right."

"You know that they're thinking of legalizing weed?"

"Oh really. Who's they?"

"The federal government."

"Frankly, I think it'll never happen," replied Audrey.

"Just wait and see sweetheart, I think you're wrong about that."

"Well, I hope you're right. Lord knows we smoke enough reefer."

"Speaking of weed, you wanna cop some soon?"

"Sure, who you thinking of getting it from, I hope it's not Bobby, the last shit we got from him was full of stems and seeds."

"I know, but I've got another connection."

"Oh yeah, who?"

"John Sommerville, he's one of Kevin's friends."

"What kind does he have?"

"Colombian red. It's some really good shit."

"Cool, then let's go for it. How much is it gonna cost us?"

"I don't know, maybe $69 or so."

"Then let's get it ASAP."

"Sure thing, sweetheart."

"Hey, you wanna have dinner with me and my folks tonight?"

"Sure, you know what your mom's cooking?"

"Don't know, but I can call her and find out."

"How's your pops doing?"

"Like I told your mom, all he seems to do is work crossword puzzles."

"He must do something else doesn't he?"

"Well yeah, he does garden quite a bit."

"What's cooking in his garden?"

"The usual, tomatoes, green beans, peas, corn, and asparagus."

Wow! I really like asparagus."

"Me too," replied Burl.

"When do you want to head their way?"

"Well not too fast, we have to finish lunch first."

"Yeah, I guess you're right."

"What about Ian? What's he gonna do?"

"I don't know, but he sure ain't coming with us."

"He'll probably have dinner with my mom or go to Fred's house and undoubtedly get stoned as shit."

"Sweetheart, you really gotta get him to chill out on smoking weed."

"I know, but the little fucker just won't stop."

"Well, all you can do is keep trying."

"Easier said than done."

"Well, you don't want him to flunk out of school do you?"

"No, my mom would get so pissed off if he did."

"There you have it."

"You think you know everything don't you?"

"No, just the important stuff."

"Sweetheart, let me call my mom and see what we're having for dinner."

"Sure thing, my love."

Burl then went into the kitchen to call his mom.

After several moments, Charlotte picked up the phone.

"Hey, Mom, what are we having for dinner?"

"One of your favorites, pepper steak."

"Mind if Audrey comes for dinner?"

"Love to have her dear."

"What time you serving dinner?"

"Probably around seven thirty."

"Want me to pick anything up on my way over?"

"If you could please go by co-op and pick up some soy sauce, that'd be helpful."

"Sure thing, Mom. Anything else?"

"Nope, that about does it."

"Great. See you later."

"Sweetheart, my mom wants us over for dinner around seven thirty."

"Great, but I first have to go home and changed into something more comfortable."

"So what's your mom fixing for dinner?"

"One of my favorites, pepper steak, you like it?"

"You better believe it. It's also one of my favorite dishes."

"Great, then let's head out to your house."

"Gotcha."

The ride in the Blue Cloud took about a half hour.

The two then entered Burl's house.

"Mom, I'm home."

"How'd school go today?"

"Pretty good."

"Burl, can I get you anything to drink?"

"No thank you, I just had something at lunch."

"Where'd you guys go?"

"Hash Brothers."

"You like the food there?"

"Sure do, their pot roast is to die for, almost better than yours.

"Just fine, you ready for lunch?"

"Sure, whatcha got?"

"Bologna, tuna fish, egg salad, ham, and turkey."

"I'll take bologna."

"How would you like it fixed?"

"Can you do fried bologna?" she asked Burl

"Sure can."

"Great. I'll have that with a little bit of mustard."

"What would you like to drink?"

"How about chocolate milk."

"Anything else?"

"How about some BBQ chips?"

"Sorry, we don't have any. How about sour cream and onion chips?"

"Yeah, that'll do."

"Coming right up."

"Mom, Burl and I are going over to his folks for dinner."

"That's fine, dear. When are you leaving?"

"Momentarily. She's serving dinner at seven thirty."

"Who's driving?"

"We're gonna be taking the Blue Cloud."

The two then headed out the door to Burl's car.

"Hop in, sweetheart."

"Okay, I will."

Burl had the Blue Cloud fixed up nicely. He'd installed a dual-barrel carburetor, leather seats, a leather steering wheel cover, and plush carpeting.

"How're doing, sweetheart?" Burl asked.

"Just fine now that I'm with you."

"Man, Audrey, you look so hot sitting in my car seat."

"You really think so?"

"Not only do I think so, I know so."

"Oh, Burl, you're so sweet."

"Only the best for my sweet love."

About fifteen minutes later, they pulled into Burl's parent's driveway.

"Here you go, sweetheart. Let's get out."

Audrey then proceeded to do so.

Sheba, their mixed-breed dog, came running out of the house.

"Come on, girl, come see me," said Burl.

Sheba jumped up on Burl and forced Burl to the ground, licking him furiously.

"That's a good girl."

"Wow! She really loves you, Burl. What breed is she?"

"Half German shepherd, half husky."

"Dear, I think that she's the sweetest dog I've ever met."

"I know, she's a real keeper. What do you say we go inside?"

"You lead the way."

They then proceeded through the garage, onto the back porch, and into the family room.

"Hey, Mom, hey, Pops, we're home."

They both appear from the living room.

"How're you two doing?" Big John asked.

"Great, Pops. How 'bout you?"

"I was just doing my crossword puzzle. Your mom was doing laundry."

"Pops, are you ever gonna give up on the crossword puzzles?"

"Nope, I find them to be very therapeutic."

"Well, whatever makes you happy."

"How goes it, Mom?"

"Fine, Burl, just finishing up some laundry."

"Need any help?" Audrey asked.

"No thanks, dear. I've got it all covered."

"If that's okay with you, I'd like to grab a seat on the back porch."

"Go right ahead, Audrey. Dinner won't be ready for about a half hour."

"Burl, you wanna join me?"

"Certainly, sweetheart."

Sheba meandered alongside Burl.

"Wow! What a beautiful day," commented Audrey.

"Sure is a day made in heaven."

"Come on girl, you wanna sit up here?" Burl said to Sheba.

The dog gladly jumped up onto the porch swing, tail wagging, tongue hanging out mouth agape.

"Sweetheart, what're your plans after graduating from Montgomery College?" Burl asked Audrey.

"I'm thinking of going to Mount St. Mary's College in Emmitsburg, Maryland. They have a good business and finance program."

"How 'bout you, dear? What are your plans?"

"Probably going to St. Mary's College in Southern Maryland, they have a great biology program."

"I'm really going to miss you, my love."

"I know, but I promise you that I'll come home every other weekend."

"It's just not the same as seeing you in person."

"Well, I know, but we'll have to make do somehow."

CHAPTER 10

Big John then entered the porch. "You two mind taking Sheba for a walk? It's a really beautiful day, and I hate to see her cooped up inside."

"Sure thing, Pops. Where's her leash?"

"It's hanging on the hook just outside the garage door."

"Audrey, would you like to go along?"

"Sure thing, dear. Just let me put my shoes on."

Audrey then grabbed her tennis shoes (Chuck Taylor) out of the Blue Cloud. "Alright, ready to go."

"See you later, Pops. We'll be home in about twenty minutes."

"Okay, son, have a good time."

"Will do, Pops." At that, Audrey and Burl set out for a leisurely stroll around the block.

"What an awesome day, Audrey."

"Like you said, truly a day made in heaven."

Twenty minutes later, they were back home.

"Let's go inside and see if we can help my mom out."

"Gotcha," replied Audrey.

"Mom, what can we do to help out?"

"If you and Audrey could please set the table, that'd be a great help."

"Sure thing, Mom. What plates would you like to use?"

"How about the Hadley? They're in the hutch in the family room."

"Audrey, could you please set the glasses on the table?"

"Sure thing, Mom, what're we having to drink?"

"You have your choice. Either lemonade, ice tea, Coca-Cola, or of course water."

"Sounds like we'll need some ice tea and maybe some lemon."

"You got it, Mom."

"Burl, could you please call your father in for dinner?"

"Sure thing, I'll get him right away."

Big John was back in the garden working away.

"Pops, time for dinner."

Big John yelled out, "Be right there, Burl."

Charlotte was just finishing up cooking the pepper steak. "Audrey, is the table set?"

"Just finished, Mom."

"Could you please help me serve up dinner? Shoot, I almost forgot the rice. Audrey, could you please heat up a pot of water for the rice?"

"Sure thing, Mom."

Burl then wandered back into the kitchen.

"Why don't we eat in the backyard on the picnic table? It's such a beautiful day. I'd hate to see it go to waste," suggested Big John.

"Good idea," replied Charlotte

The weather was your typical September evening—midseventies in temperature and low relative humidity.

"Audrey, could you please help me serve up dinner?" Charlotte asked.

"Sure, Mom. Wow! This pepper steak looks so delicious," replied Audrey.

"I second that," Burl said.

"Looking really good," replied Big John.

At that, the four of them headed out to the backyard with Sheba in tow.

"Okay, who'd like to say grace?" asked Charlotte.

"I'll do the honors," replied Big John. He then proceeded to recite the grace. "Dear God, our Heavenly Father, please bless this food to our loving use and to the hands that prepared it. Amen."

"Let's dig in!" replied Burl. And that they did.

Forty-five minutes later, they had finished their meal.

"Mom, you really outdid yourself on the meal. It was delicious," said Audrey.

"I agree," replied Burl.

"Now, how about dessert?" Charlotte inquires.

"I don't know, Mom, I'm full," replied Big John.

"Then how about something light like strawberry Jell-O topped with whipped cream?" suggested Charlotte.

"Sounds good to me," replied Burl.

"I'll have the same. Audrey responded.

"Me too," replied Big John.

"Okay then, who'd like to help me serve dessert?" asked Charlotte.

"I'll help you out, Mom," replied Audrey.

"Great, then we're all set," responded Charlotte.

Audrey and Charlotte then headed into the kitchen to retrieve the desserts.

"Audrey, the parfait cups are in the cupboard above the refrigerator. If you could please get them down."

"Sure, Mom."

"Also, if you could grab the whipped cream and Jell-O out of the fridge, that'd be a great help."

"Gotcha, Mom."

Audrey then proceeded to carry out her chore.

"Let's serve up," said Charlotte.

"Gotcha covered, Mom."

The two of them served up the dessert in the parfait cups and then headed out to the picnic table.

"Here you go, fellas. Desserts on!"

"I'm glad that we decided on something light," said Burl.

"Me too," replied Big John.

"I second that," replied Audrey.

"So what's on the horizon for you two lovebirds in the future?" Charlotte asked.

"Audrey and I are graduating this spring from Montgomery College with our associate's degree."

"Wow! You two must be very excited," replied Charlotte.

"Yeah, we are," Audrey and Burl said in unison.

They all finished their desserts in about a half hour.

"Man, I'm really beat," said Burl. "You mind if Audrey sleeps over tonight?"

"No problem," replied Charlotte. "She can sleep in the room across the hallway from your room." At that point, they crash out for the night.

Summer bled into fall, fall into winter, and winter into spring. Time for graduation.

Both Burl and Audrey graduated with high honors. Burl pursued his bachelor's degree in biology at St. Mary's College as planned and ultimately enrolled in a graduate program at UMBC (University of Maryland, Baltimore County). Discouraged, he left the program and pursued a career in entomology at the University of Maryland, College Park. He then pursued a career at microbiological associates in Rockville, Maryland, as a laboratory technician. He finally ended up working for the Mid-Atlantic Laboratory Equipment Company, selling lab products to the pharmaceutical and biotech industries.

Audrey on the other hand, pursued her degree in business and finance as planned at Mount St. Mary's College. She graduated Summa cum laude with a 4.0 grade point average. She was smart as a whip.

Following her graduation from the Mount, she worked with several IT firms in sales, marketing, and business development where she became highly successful. She obtained high accolades from senior executives within these companies.

On May 18, 1985, Burl and Audrey would get married at St. Mary's church in Rockville by Monsignor Costick. It was a splendid occasion, no holds barred.

On April 23, 1990, Audrey would give birth to Andrew Ian (a.k.a. Drew Beatz), a fine young lad.

On July 28, 1999, Audrey would give birth to Phillip Dennis, also a fine young man.

Unfortunately, Phillip would die from a horrendous car accident while en route to a family vacation over a Thanksgiving holiday. Burl was rear-ended by a pickup truck that crushed Burl's Toyota Corolla to pieces while he was driving, Phillip was in the passenger seat. As it turned out, both Phillip and Burl had to be removed from Burl's car by the jaws of life. Burl was told by the doctors that he had severe bleeding in the brain and was put on a ventilator for four weeks.

Phillip was also ventilated for a period but to no avail. The last time Burl and Audrey saw their sweet angel Phil was when they were holding his hands as his precious life slowly ebbed away. Talk about a messed-up situation, this was the absolute worst. Phillip passed on April 25, 2020, coincidentally, Charlotte's birthday.

Burl and Audrey eventually moved to a home in Germantown, Maryland. with their two children. The home was a paradise of sorts. It was equipped with a sauna a hot tub and a swimming pool and landscaped to the hilt. Life was so beautiful then except for Audrey's passing on January 7, 2021, due to a stroke. Burl and Andrew held Audrey in their arms as she passed away. She was airlifted to Fairfax Inova Hospital in Fairfax, Virginia, where she breathed her last breath.

Pressured to move out of his Germantown home, Burl eventually moved to Leisure World, a retirement community in Silver Spring, Maryland. Ultimately, Burl did not regret the move. The community had a golf course, a woodshop and was a stone's throw away from restaurants and grocery stores as well as his Catholic church, Our Lady of Grace. It also had the added benefit of being close to other family members.

All in all, Burl was very happy with his living condition.

In the meantime, Andrew would move to Thurmont, Maryland, with his Siberian husky, Kodei, along with his good friend Frank (a.k.a. the Cuban).

At the time of writing this manuscript, Burl was sixty-four years old and would be sixty-nine in five more years and very much alive.

The End

ABOUT THE AUTHOR

Burl Sorenson was born and raised in Rockville, Maryland, and in subsequent years attended St. Mary's College of Maryland where he received his BS in biology.

Although Burl doesn't have journalistic experience, he draws his knowledge and experience from writing extensively during his attendance at St. Mary's.

In his own words, "My writing is strongly influenced by my unwavering faith in God my Father and my Lord Jesus Christ and inspiration from my deceased wife, Sheila, and deceased son, Phillip. May they rest in peace."

Burl currently resides in Silver Spring, Maryland, along with his cat, Simba.